## Advance Praise for *Wetwork Repair*

"I served with Bill when he was a senior executive at the CIA where he was a rock star. You will ask yourself if this book is based on fact or fiction and maybe even prophecy. Read for enjoyment, but don't expect it to put you to sleep at night. It will stimulate you to do some serious pondering of the story line. A great read!"

—Lt. Gen. (Ret.) William G. Boykin,
US Army

"My friend, retired CIA officer, Bill Rooney has the guts to touch a raw nerve. What's in this book could very well happen here. You and President Trump need to read it now, before it happens!"

—Former NRA President
t.)
es

William Rooney

# WETWORK REPAIR

PERMUTED
PRESS

A PERMUTED PRESS BOOK
ISBN: 978-1-68261-864-6
ISBN (eBook): 978-1-68261-865-3

Wetwork Repair
© 2019 by William Rooney
All Rights Reserved

Cover art by Jim Vranas of Create4Corners

**PERMUTED**
PRESS

Permuted Press, LLC
New York • Nashville
permutedpress.com

Published in the United States of America

To the distinguished retired CIA officers in the Malbec Group. You have done a lot to defend this country. Thanks for your service.

# CHAPTER ONE

An overcast gray sky had settled on the North Carolina countryside. It had just stopped raining heavily the night before, and the grounds throughout the cemetery remained wet and muddy. It was early autumn and the temperature for the day was expected only to reach the mid-forties.

A number of rubber mats had been placed strategically on the grass in the cemetery between the access road and the burial site. They were there to assist people who parked and got out of their vehicles to walk single file up to the grave site. The mats were themselves already wet and muddy but certainly a better option than walking on the deep, drenched, and slippery grass.

About forty yards in stood a group of twenty-five or more people on the periphery of a large blue tarpaulin-topped tent supported by aluminum poles and covering two caskets. Under the tarpaulin sat two women on metal chairs positioned directly along the side of the caskets, which lay next to each other, separated only by one of the rubber mats. A US flag lay over the top of each casket. Two teenage boys sat next to the woman on the right side. The women and the young boys all had their heads down listening to a clergyman standing in front of them. The clergyman was leaning in and speaking in hushed tones to the four of them. The woman with the kids kept shaking her head as if in disbelief. The oldest boy put his hand on her shoulder to help but there was little he or his brother could do. Both widows were crying and dabbing with handkerchiefs at the tears rolling down their faces.

After several minutes, the clergyman stopped talking to them and stood up straight. He walked around to the other side of the caskets where he stopped and turned toward the gathering. In a loud, commanding voice the clergyman recited prayers and final blessings.

"Isaiah 43:2—Going over the Mountain. 'When you pass through the waters, I will be with you, and through the rivers, they will not overwhelm you. When you walk through the fire, you will not be burned or scorched, nor will the flame kindle upon you.'"

He concluded by making the sign of the cross and lowering his head. There was complete silence.

To the surprise of some, a man off to the side of the assembled mourners raised a bugle and played *Taps*. Most had not seen the musician arrive and take up his position. All heads were bowed. A number of those gathered were crying.

A funeral home official announced, "Family, friends, and relatives are now invited to come up and pay their last respects."

The mourners walked single file up to the immediate family members and expressed their condolences, then slowly walked past the caskets saying final prayers. Many of them cried, shaking their heads and placing a flower on the caskets. They then stepped back onto the wet mats to return to their vehicles.

The last people approaching to pay their respects were six men in black suits and ties. Three of them wore unbuttoned raincoats. They were fit and athletic and varied in size and weight. All had long hair and two had full-grown dark beards. They all appeared solemn.

Each of the six men individually expressed his condolences to the wives and two sons of the deceased. Thereafter, each made it a point to thank the clergyman for his words and prayers. Next, one by one, each of the six men walked up to the first casket and placed a hand on the American flag still covering it. Each bowed his head in silent prayer before moving to the second casket and doing the same.

The last of the six men wore an open raincoat, but as he stopped in front of the first casket he reached inside the coat and across his chest with his right hand to pull out from an inside pocket a green beret. He placed the beret on his head and then bowed. A moment later he lifted his head and snapped a salute over the casket. He slowly brought his saluting hand down before stepping over to the next casket and repeating his bow and salute. As he stepped back to return to the cars, he removed his beret and placed it back inside his coat under his left arm. He made no eye contact with anyone as he walked away.

Back on the access road, down to the far right, away from the other vehicles, stood the other five men behind a Chevy pickup truck. The tailgate of the truck was down, and one of the men was handing out cold beers from an ice chest to each in the group. He opened a bottle and handed it to the last of the six men. No one had taken a drink. They waited until the six of them had a beer in their hand. No one spoke.

The man with the beret tucked in his raincoat lifted his bottle to the heavens and said, "Rest peacefully, brothers, and God bless America!"

The others raised their beers and chorused, "Amen! God bless America!"

They drank their beers before exchanging bear hugs and handshakes. Several of them made quick work of their first beer and went over to the cooler for a second.

The six stayed together until the family and relatives had departed the cemetery. After saying their good-byes to each other, the six quietly started toward their respective cars and trucks. Two of them, the two who were parked the farthest away, walked together.

"When did'ja get in?"

"Just this morning. How'd it go last night?"

"Pretty rough, as you can imagine. One open casket and one closed. The wives and kids had a real bad time but there was a good turnout at the funeral parlor. They've got a lot of local support around them, but it's still going to be tough. Many of the folks who were at last night's viewing explained to me that they couldn't be here today 'cause they are working. Folks work hard for their money around these parts. Still, I counted maybe twenty-five or so here today."

They walked in silence for several minutes before one of them looked over to the other and said, "I'm going to miss them. They'll always be remembered."

"I hope so, but you'd be amazed at how quickly some people forget. That's a crying shame…and that crying shame pisses me off."

# CHAPTER TWO

S tephen Craig put his feet on the cool wooden floor of the upstairs master bedroom at 5:15 a.m. He rose and went over to his walk-in closet, turned on the light, dressed, picked up his shoes, and tiptoed carefully downstairs to the kitchen, trying not to wake anyone in the house. In the kitchen he put on and tied his shoes before having a quick breakfast of cereal, juice, and coffee. After he took his dishes over to the sink, he slipped on a Gore-Tex windbreaker, picked up his sport jacket, tie, and attaché case, and went out the front door to his driveway, where he got into his brand-new top-of-the-line BMW. It was late autumn and temperatures were dropping.

At 5:50 a.m. he eased out of the driveway into the pitch-black morning with the only light coming from his low-beam headlights.

Stephen Craig hated Mondays, and today was Monday.

He worked for the *Washington Gazette Bugle*, the leading Washington, DC, city newspaper in circulation. Critics of the newspaper viewed the *Bugle* as a left-leaning rag and a field artillery piece of propaganda delivering never-ending partisan attacks on Republicans and conservatives. They argued that the *Bugle*'s story line was carefully molded to conform to the cookie-cutter policies of the Democratic party and the progressives' agenda. They believed all *Bugle* stories to be filtered through the leftist agenda before being published, and whatever the story dealt with, it clearly and usually carried a sharp critical cutting edge against the stance and stated position of the opposition Republican party.

It seemed to many that newspapers and TV news shows had become propaganda arms of their respective political parties. Attack your political opponent whenever possible...and if attacked or counterattacked, downplay or even bury their charges against you. To state that the *Gazette Bugle* was a partisan tool was a gross understatement. These same critics viewed the newspaper's hypocrisy as limitless, and claimed the *Gazette Bugle* was all about "spin" and a Democratic party win in the next elections. They pointed out that, whenever caught flat-footed in stating a mistruth or lie, the *Gazette Bugle* simply claimed that the Republicans had done the same thing, or far worse.

Editors at the *Gazette Bugle* never hesitated to tell their readers whom they should vote for in national, state, or municipal elections, and were no less opinionated about world leaders and events. They urged electoral support for their own "chosen ones" and undercut and attacked anyone or anything in the opposition. Not surprisingly, the newspaper's brand was wrapped in the claim and veneer of "independent journalism." Those at the newspaper denied they were wearing team arm bands, team colors, and team insignias on their team hats. "Independent" and "journalism" were the two operative words consistently used when the newspaper was promoting its reporting. Yet many fair questions could be raised by their critics about both the words "independent" and "journalism."

Stephen Craig was one of the *Gazette Bugle*'s rising stars. His articles appeared weekly and he had become a regular guest on various weekend TV news talk programs. A number of his front-page stories were sourced to highly placed US government officials. These sources many times carried the disclaimer of "anonymous," as the individuals were not authorized to discuss publicly the matters contained in the articles.

Craig's large ego was only outdone by his ambition. He knew well he was a rising star at the newspaper and that the *Gazette Bugle* viewed him as their go-to guy on sensitive world events. He was becoming more and more famous. He had just had his fourth book published on world events and what he thought was wrong with US foreign policy.

Craig did not have a good reputation among his fellow workers, who viewed him to be overly ambitious and a cut-throat social climber. Not a team player, he viewed himself as the real "star." It was always about him and his notoriety. He knew he was on his way up and his fellow workers knew better than to stand in his way.

Behind his back the other reporters referred to him as "T. F. Craig," a shorthand version of "That F-ing Craig." When he was not present in the office people would come up and ask, "When's T. F. coming in?" or "Where's T. F.?"

If Craig was aware of this derogatory office label, he never made any effort to change his style or work habits. He knew he was the star, and those demeaning him were wasting their time. They simply were not important.

Craig and his family lived in Potomac, Maryland. He traveled daily back and forth to the newspaper by car. What he hated about the commute was traffic, especially morning traffic on River Road. Speed cameras were everywhere, and if you did not leave your home by at least 6:00 a.m.

you risked being tied up in heavy traffic. River Road was always congested during rush hours going into Washington. At night Craig sometimes would delay departure from his office until 7:00 or 7:30 p.m., and even then he might run into traffic delays.

It was really dark on his street when Craig pulled out of his driveway onto his cul-de-sac and drove toward the corner where he would make a left turn onto the feeder road to River Road.

As he neared the end of his street to make his turn, he glanced to his right and saw a man in his headlights standing on the corner with a dog on a leash. He had never before seen this person or his dog out walking at this early hour. He thought to himself that this guy had to be cold, being out there in these falling late-autumn temperatures. The guy did have on a long coat and a pulled-down hat but he looked uncomfortable and certainly had to be chilled.

Craig slowed as he neared the corner and intended to let the guy and his dog cross before he made his turn. In his headlights he saw the guy wave him on to go ahead. As Craig rounded the corner, the guy held up his hand to show he appreciated the courtesy.

Only moments after Craig turned onto the feeder road, he looked ahead out to the end of his headlight beams and saw what appeared to be a large SUV stopped and situated diagonally across the middle of the road. The feeder road was two blocks from River Road and ran parallel to a golf course on the right side and several expensive homes set back behind trees and shrubs on the left. As Craig drove up, a guy got out of the SUV and gestured to him as if he wanted him to stop. Craig pulled up thinking the guy was going to ask him if he had jumper cables. Craig had them but he was not going to jump-start any car with his expensive new BMW.

The guy approached his front car door and Craig opened his window.

"Morning, I see you've got a problem. I don't have jumper cables." Craig did not even blink telling the lie.

The guy blew into his hands. "Nope, I'm okay, but there's a problem ahead near the River Road intersection. Don't need jumper cables but I'm wondering if there is another way we can get out to the main drag."

Both men turned when another man asked, "What's going on?"

It was the dog walker and his leashed dog. With the window down Craig was beginning to feel the morning chill, as was the SUV driver who again was blowing into his cold hands.

"Seems there's some kind of problem ahead down near River Road," Craig said.

"I can check," said the dog walker, who, with his free hand, reached into his now unbuttoned coat as if he was going to get out his cell phone.

The dog walker pulled out a large magnum pistol and pointed it directly at Craig's head. "Mr. Craig, make no sudden moves or you will be a dead man. My friend and I are here to talk to you, so get out of the car slowly and don't do anything stupid."

"Who the hell are you guys?" Craig sputtered. "I don't have money on me. But if you're after money we can go to an ATM and I'll give you what you want. Don't hurt me… please. And how do you know my name?"

"This is not about money, Mr. Craig, so please step out of the car and follow my friend to the SUV. We only want to talk with you today and you'll understand things a lot better after we've had our chat."

Craig got out of his car, staring intently at the gun in the dog walker's hand. He stood up and raised his hands. "All right, all right, take it easy."

"Put your hands down, Mr. Craig. This is not a John Wick movie. Get over to the SUV and do what you're told."

"What about my car? I can't just leave it here in the middle of the street."

"We'll take care of it, don't worry. After you've heard what we want to say, you'll be back driving it to work."

By this time another man had gotten out of the SUV still diagonally parked in front of the BMW. He approached them.

"Jaime, get into Mr. Craig's car and follow us," the dog walker said to the third man. "Please drive carefully, because it's brand new and Mr. Craig has had it for only three months and twelve days. It's his pride and joy."

Craig walked to the SUV with the SUV driver on his one side and the dog and the dog walker on the other side. The dog walker still had the gun in his hand but was now carrying it down by his side.

Who the hell were these guys, how did they know his name, where he lived, what time he left for work, and when he'd bought his car?

Craig shook his head.

"Get in, Mr. Craig, and put on the rubber face mask you'll find when you get into the back seat. You'll have no problem breathing through the mask but you'll not be able to see out of it. Sit quietly until we get to our destination. I'll be right next to you. I'm putting the dog in the back so don't be startled if he barks."

Craig did as he was told and got in. He was scared and his heart was racing. He couldn't stop thinking about the large gun that had been aimed at his forehead. He didn't think he had ever before seen any one of the three men, and he wondered how their paths could have crossed. He had no idea what this was all about.

The inside of the SUV smelled new. The dog walker handed him the rubber mask and helped him adjust it after he had put it on. He could not see a thing but he had no trouble breathing.

The powerful SUV engine started and they soon were on their way. They drove with no one in the SUV talking for maybe twenty or thirty minutes, making any number of turns while varying speeds. Craig surmised this was all meant to confuse him about being on highways or back roads. The ominous silence was broken only now and then by the dog walker telling the driver to make a left or right turn. Everything became a blur in Craig's mind. He gave up trying to figure anything about where they might be, what road they might be on, or where they might be taking him. Instead, he kept asking himself, *Who are these guys?*

They finally made a stop and one of the SUV doors opened. A moment later Craig thought he heard a garage door opening. The SUV rolled forward and stopped. Then Craig heard what he was now sure was a garage door closing.

Craig still had the rubber mask on when he was taken out of the vehicle and escorted, one person on each side of him, into whatever building it was they were entering.

No one spoke. Craig was helped into a chair and then his mask removed. The brightness in the room forced him to first close his eyes, then blink and squint.

After a moment he was able to focus and look around. He was sitting at the end of a dining room table that could seat eight persons, looking directly at the dog walker who was at the other end of the table. No one else appeared to be still in the room. It was just the two of them. On the table to Craig's right sat a DVD player and thirty-inch TV that had a blank screen but was already turned on. The dog walker had removed his topcoat and now sat at the table in a black sports jacket and turtleneck.

His hat was on the table to the left and his magnum sat close by to his right hand, which he rested on the tabletop.

"Mr. Craig, please take off your coat and try to relax. We're here to talk with you, not to hurt you. If we only wanted to hurt you or kill you, we could've easily done that already. I'm going to ask you to listen carefully to what I've got to say to you today, so pay close attention."

The dog walker removed his hat from the table and put it on the chair to his right. His weapon stayed right where it was next to his right hand. His voice remained steady and calm.

"To make what I'm going to say to you clearer, I'm going to show you two short DVDs that'll set the stage for our discussion. Watch these short clips carefully and we'll talk with you later about them. Jaime," he called, "come on in and turn on the first DVD."

As Jaime came in and started the DVD, the dog walker said, "This first footage was shot in Central America some years ago. You'll quickly get the picture. By the way, this actually happened. You'll be looking at the real thing."

The DVD started and footage shot from a camera located off the side of a road showed a car coming up a barren road on a bright summer day. Two men sat in the car with all the windows down. The camera coverage shifted to the rear of the car and showed a dark green pickup truck with a tarpaulin covering the truck's short bed coming up fast, as if to pass it. Both vehicles were now in the picture and the truck was blinking its lights, indicating it wanted to pass. The driver in the car stuck his arm out the open window and waved the pickup truck on. The DVD camera footage was then spliced so that the filming was now being taken from the front seat of the truck coming up to pass. The camera in the truck stayed on the car as the truck swung out and came up on the left and around to pass. The camera zoomed in on the face of the car driver, who had his left arm out waving the truck to come on by. As the truck went by the left front door of the car, the truck tarpaulin suddenly was thrown off and two men stood up with submachine guns and fired directly into the car. Glass and blood splattered everywhere, arms and bodies jerked awkwardly upward and sideways. The car abruptly swerved off the road and came to a stop in an open field.

The next camera footage had been spliced to show up-close filming of the damage done to the occupants in the car. The man in the passenger seat was slumped against the closed right car door, his mouth and eyes wide open. The driver was slumped over the wheel with his bloody head pulled back by the cameraman to show a number of grotesque head wounds from the machine guns. The footage was spliced to show the car on fire and burning in a field with the two dead bodies in it.

Craig felt confused and sickened, wondering what this all had to do with him.

The dog walker picked up on his apparent confusion. "This will get a lot clearer in a moment or two, Mr. Craig, after we show you our next DVD."

Jaime, if that really was his name, came into the room and replaced the first DVD. The dog walker nodded and Jaime pushed the play button.

Craig looked at the screen and was shocked to see his wife in a short tennis outfit getting out of her car and walking back to the open trunk where their two kids were seen waiting to put their bags into the trunk. His wife and kids appeared to be greeting each other but there was no sound on the DVD. His wife was talking to both of them as his son put two large bags into the trunk. His daughter followed and stepped up to put in a bag of her own along with a school knapsack. His wife closed the trunk and the three got in the car and drove off. There was no indication that any one of them knew or had even a hint or slightest suspicion that they were being filmed. Everything appeared natural and innocent.

"Your wife is very pretty," the dog walker said, "and I suspect a good bit younger than you. Your son has your features and your daughter has your wife's good looks. Your son seems happy at his college and we understand your daughter is seriously considering going to journalism school. But perhaps I am being too coy, Mr. Craig. The point I want you to understand is that we know all we need to know about your family members and their schedules."

Craig was shocked to see his wife and kids appear so vulnerable. They had no idea they were being watched let alone filmed. They were oblivious and unaware of any danger.

In the same steady and calm voice the dog walker said, "But maybe I'm being too polite here, Mr. Craig, so let me make a stark point to get your full attention by adding that some in my group are eager to find out if Mrs. Craig would be as good in bed as she looks in that short tennis skirt. And a couple of the younger guys even complimented your daughter's appearance."

The dog walker let that sink in and took a moment before continuing.

"Excuse me please, that's crass of me, but I wanted to make the point that we're not always polite in what we do, think, or say."

In a low, frightened voice Craig asked, "What do you want from me?"

"Ah yes, I like that, Mr. Craig. Let's get down to business. Now that we've got your attention, listen carefully to what I'm going to say. We've read all of your newspaper articles and faithfully watch your appearances on the talk shows. A couple of us have even read your pontificating books about failed US policy. You're a real man-about-town. We notice with great interest how many times you leak, or come close to leaking, a story or comment on something that clearly is classified information. In fact, when you've been challenged on three occasions in the last two years by underlings at the Justice Department implying you were revealing classified information, you've pictured yourself as strapping on the helmet, picking up the sword, and lifting the shield of liberty to be a champion who is going to risk even going to jail before revealing your source of any classified information. You've portrayed yourself as a hero wrapped in the First Amendment and constitutional protections about freedom of the press and freedom of speech. 'Send me to jail, but I will not reveal my sources.' We've watched with interest as you've defended these actions with arguments that the American people had a right to know this information. If only you were as aggressive and interested in defending national security. Instead, your focus has been only on working your sources and getting a scoop on the next big behind-the-scenes government issue. Your approach is 'We have no secrets.' You pay no attention to secrecy laws and promote your articles with a salesman pitch of 'You won't believe this story from my secret source.' We've become convinced your reporting is only about you and your career, and you being a big celebrity here in Washington. It's not about you leaking classified information, breaking laws, or endangering national security. I guess you think secrecy is 'old think' and not needed in our new super-tech age. But then, why would you care, if it helps promote your career?"

Craig was shaking his head in disagreement.

"Wait, Mr. Craig," the dog walker said. "I've got more to say, and then you'll better understand my message to you today.

"Several weeks ago you broke a big story about a clandestine covert-action black-op unfolding in Yemen where special-ops guys and tier-one operatives were planning to target high-level terrorist leaders. Your source for this classified information was, of course, unnamed, with you stating in your story only that this well-placed 'anonymous' official was unauthorized to comment publicly on the story. Your story hinted strongly that these high-level targets were going to be assassinated and that the targets were Shia and close affiliates of Iranian government Shia officials. You made no mention, however, that the actual targets in the operation were, and still are, terrorists who are planning to kill every American in our embassy in Sana. Your story revealed this to be a joint Saudi-US operation aimed at Iran and Iranian supporters in Yemen. You implied that the US claim that it was fighting terrorism in this case was a subterfuge to strike a blow against Iran and their supporting Shia elements in Yemen. The Yemeni targets, meanwhile, were portrayed as innocent victims in the sniper scopes of US black-op assassination teams. No hint of the targets being cold-blooded terrorist killers who would kill any infidel in front of them. You raised the question as to whether this operation, if carried out, would draw the United States further into the Saudi strategy and religious war between the Shia and Sunni now unfolding in the region. You also asked if the operation would result in US troops having to deploy to Yemen. Then you raised the question whether the US public was being duped, lied to, and misled."

The dog walker shook his head and took a deep breath. He looked directly into Craig's eyes. "The same day you broke the story on the front page of the *Gazette Bugle*, the operation, which was aimed at taking out a number of high-level terrorists, was abruptly stopped, and the operatives who were doing the targeting were told to stand down."

The dog walker stood up and called to one of his men to bring in some coffee and Danish. He gestured for his accomplice to put the coffee cups in front of them and the Danish to the left of Craig. There must have been a dozen pastries in a cardboard box from Starbucks, along with paper plates, napkins, and two coffees in large paper cups.

"You will find your coffee exactly the way you like it, Mr. Craig. Two sugars and a splash of half-and-half."

He picked up his own coffee cup and took a drink. "What you don't know is that we lost two highly skilled operatives in this targeting action, two guys who risked everything to defend American national security. How they died makes the drive-by DVD from Central America you just saw look like a water balloon fight. Two good guys dead, bad guys gone to ground and now deeper in hiding, and Americans in Yemen in greater danger than ever before. Iranian and Yemeni newspapers are having a field day about the US and Saudi Arabian plans to come in and kill innocent Shia leaders. More points on the scoreboard for Iran and Shia terrorists.

"Meanwhile, here in the capital, you and your 'deep source' of this classified information went about your business as if nothing had happened. No one took you to task for leaking the information, and no one implied that your leak was treason. Not one hint in your article that mounting the operation must have taken great sacrifice, risk, and time. There certainly was no mention of losing the two black-op operators who really were true patriots. All efforts to mount the operation to kill these terrorists were for naught. We were told to go back to the drawing board because this operation was in a complete stand-down. It became too politically hot to continue. All of this because of your front-page article from your 'secret source.'"

# CHAPTER THREE

**C**raig cleared his throat and took a gulp of coffee and asked, "Who the hell are you guys? Are you Agency? Delta? DEVGRU? Marine Raiders? Are you contractors from a Beltway bandit outfit? Who *are* you?"

"Who we are, Mr. Craig, is your worst nightmare, and that's not a line out of a movie, trust me. Friends of the two patriots we lost are asking themselves why you had to run the story. They also want to know who the source is who gave you the story, and why, after so much work had already been done to mount the operation, you and your source leaked it when you did. They want to ask if you gave any thought whatsoever to the safety of those out there in the sandbox facing the everyday terrorist threat and putting their lives on the line to defend our national security. They want some answers, Mr. Craig. They're extremely unhappy."

Craig shook his head. "Hey, look, I wasn't trying to put anyone in danger, and I certainly didn't know about the two dead operatives. If my source knew, he didn't tell me. My editors and I broke the story because we were worried about mission creep in Yemen. We didn't want the United States to get sucked into a regional religious war between Iran and Saudi Arabia. If we killed Shia political leaders in Yemen, who, as you pointed out, are closely associated with Iran, there certainly would have been pushback and more killing from their side. I felt the American public needed to know and we had to go into this danger with our eyes open. I asked myself if our so-called war on terrorism gave us the right to target anyone, anywhere. I also was troubled by the word 'target,' which I interpreted in this case to mean 'kill or assassinate,' and I wondered who in government had the authority to make such a decision without the public knowing? I did not know about your two operators."

The dog walker nodded, as if he had taken in and understood all Craig had to say. "Mr. Craig, do you really think, given your experience in international affairs, that our target selection was random and made only to piss off the Iranians? Our targets were and still are terrorist killers who would eagerly put you on camera and have you plead for your life before slashing your throat. As you gagged on your own blood and died with your eyes wide open, they would be reading a warning to infidels to get out of the Middle East. They would then sever your head and lift it up to the camera for all to see.

"And do you think for a minute that if you were a newspaper reporter in Sana or Teheran and you revealed operational information about an upcoming planned attack on Americans that you would live to see the sun rise the next day? But you live here in America where very little remains classified and there are no secrets other than the names of people leaking classified information to the press."

The eyes of the dog walker were fixed on Craig. "In your world, your byline and newspaper circulation appear to drive the train, and national security trails far behind. So, Mr. Craig, have a pastry and drink your coffee because I am now going to tell you exactly what we want and what we are going to do to get what we want."

The dog walker got up with his pistol in his right hand and stepped over to get a pastry. He stood only a foot and a half from Craig and looked directly into his eyes before shifting his gaze to the box of pastries. He selected one and put it on a paper plate. He took a napkin, walked back to the other end of table, and sat down. His weapon was placed back on the table near his right hand. He said nothing as he slowly ate his pastry and drank more of his coffee. At least three or four minutes went by before the dog walker wiped his lips with a napkin and he looked at Craig.

"Mr. Craig, you hardly touched your coffee and didn't even try the Danish. But I understand the circumstances and know you are somewhat upset about meeting me today. So allow me to get right to the point, Mr. Craig. Who is your informant? Who leaked the classified information to you on Yemen? Is it a he or is it a she? Does the source work in the Agency, or perhaps in the Pentagon, or somewhere else in the intelligence community? We want a name, Mr. Craig, and you're going to give it to us.

"Save yourself the trouble of shaking your head. You're going to tell us the name of your source after you've had time to think about what you'll lose if you don't give us what we want. It's not going to be a tough decision to make after you realize what we will do if you don't cooperate."

Craig sat up straighter in his chair. "You know I can't reveal my source! I've stood before a judge in the past and told him I'd go to jail before giving up a source's name. This is about freedom of the press and the right of the American public to know the truth. It is about our Constitution and American core values."

"Please, please, Mr. Craig, save the speech for someone who's interested. Now listen carefully about a deal we're offering you today, a deal that only you and I will know about."

The dog walker called for Jaime, who came into the room and approached the table.

"Jaime, please run the DVD from Central America and then the second one with his wife and kids. Mr. Craig, watch carefully. I'll be right back to talk with you after you watch the DVDs and after I've made a pit stop."

He got up and walked out of the room. Jaime pushed the play button, then walked to the front of the room where Craig could see him.

Craig was more alert watching the footage the second time around now that the initial shock had worn off. His mind was clearer and he saw much more detail in the film. The two targets in the car had no idea they would be shot dead in the seconds it took the truck to pass. The close-ups of the torn-apart chests, heads, and faces of the victims were sickening, and the photographer doing the filming seemed to keep the camera focused on the deadly wounds longer than needed. Craig was still absorbing the brutality in the first DVD when he watched his wife and kids meeting in a parking lot at a mall and loading packages into his wife's car. How could they not have known they were being filmed? The DVD ended with something new that had not been shown the first time around. It was a scene of a gravesite in an empty cemetery with four headstones.

Jaime clicked off the DVD player and closed it as the dog walker came back in and sat down.

Craig's stomach felt queasy. "I think I'm going to be sick. Can I have a glass of water?"

"Jaime, would you please get a glass of water for Mr. Craig?"

When Jaime returned, the dog walker allowed Craig to take two unhurried sips of water before speaking.

"Mr. Craig, let me borrow a line used by Colombian drug traffickers when they want to make a deal with someone: You lie, you die. This is understood by Colombians to mean if you lie, you and your family will die. That is generally not the sequence of events, because the family is usually targeted and taken out in front of the person not cooperating. The drug kingpins usually tell the person involved that he is responsible for killing his family and there is no more reason for him to live. Then they kill him.

"Mr. Craig, you clearly have a lot to lose. But let me be more specific. You will lose your wife and kids, and then your own life, in that order. Now, if you give us the information we want, you can go on your way and neither you nor any family member gets hurt. Only you will know that you gave us a name. Your source will never find out. If you give us a name and then go out and warn this person, or if you give us a name and then run to the Feds, we'll know and you and your family will be sorry sooner or later. Take a few minutes to think this proposal over. If you don't make the right decision, your wife and kids will be targeted this same morning when she has them both in the car and is dropping them off at the high school and Metro station. They will be killed before they get to either location. We'll film the killings and show it to you right here on the DVD. Your house is already under surveillance and we know on Monday mornings they usually leave at 7:55 a.m. Our pickup truck with shooters under the tarpaulin is already in place just down from where the SUV was parked this morning. They will have no idea before it's too late."

The dog walker paused, then added, "So we now only await your decision. Oh, and save me from all the 'I couldn't live with myself' hand-wringing. We are running out of time, Mr. Craig, so I have to ask you for the name of your source. I'm only going to ask one last time: Who is your source? If you don't tell me in the next two minutes I will make a call to the shooters right here in front of you. After that, you'll see a video of the victims before I personally put a bullet into your chest. It isn't a hard decision to make, Mr. Craig, believe me."

Craig was wide-eyed. "What will you do to him if I give you his name?"

"We will talk privately with him and convince him that his actions are harming national security. You have my word that we'll try to make him understand our position and convince him not to repeat his mistake of leaking any more classified information. Your name will never be mentioned and he'll think perhaps someone inside government circles began to suspect him. We'll cover your tracks completely."

Craig drew in a big breath and then looked up at the dog walker. In a trembling voice he said, "Ed Pierce."

"Repeat that, Mr. Craig. Did you say Ed Pierce? Ed Pierce from the Agency? Did I hear you right? Speak up, Mr. Craig!"

Craig nodded. "Yes, Ed Pierce from the Agency."

Craig had great respect for Ed Pierce and knew him to be a subject-matter expert on the Middle East and a really good guy who for many recent years has been uneasy with the US Saudi policy and its failure to address the spread of Wahhabism teachings throughout Arab schools. He viewed Wahhabism as spreading anti-American propaganda, depicting Westerners as infidels, and undercutting American foreign policy in the region. He considered it a Saudi extremist doctrine that allowed the Saudis to play both sides in the terrorism debate.

"He came to me with the story because he thought the Saudis were leading us down a dangerous path that risked America becoming ensnared in a high-risk, sure-to-lose gamble," Craig explained. "Pierce was trying to save American lives and treasure. That was why he didn't want us to support the Saudi gambit." Craig paused a moment. "Pierce is a patriot. Please don't hurt him. He was trying to do the right thing. He didn't want us to be duped by the Saudis!"

"Is he your only source, Mr. Craig?"

"Yes, he is my only source. I took the gist of his story and went around to my network of government contacts for confirmation and additional information. I knew I had something big when one of my contacts in the Pentagon told me to tread carefully because I was walking in a minefield. I avoided contacting anyone in the Agency to confirm my information for fear I would raise suspicions. For the most part, I ran into blind alleys and got little additional information. I even went back to Ed Pierce to tell him I was getting little to corroborate his story, and he doubled down and gave me more detail about the most recent Saudi-US meetings and plans to take action in Yemen. He repeated his view that the Saudis were walking us into a trap. That's when my editors and I decided we needed to get the story out quickly, which we did.

"Look, I told you the truth. Please don't hurt my family. I've given you Ed's name but will tell you he was trying to save American lives. I knew nothing about your two operatives being killed. If you have any doubts about what I've told you, put a bullet in me right now, but I beg you, please leave my family alone."

"Take it easy, Mr. Craig," the dog walker said calmly. "You answered my question. If you are playing any games, we can always reach back and contact you. Tell no one of today's meeting. Your name will never come up in our discussions with Pierce. Our mission is not to kill US citizens but to protect our country. Meanwhile, and this is a warning, publish your next story based on classified information at your own risk."

The dog walker stood up from the table. "You'll now be taken back to pick up your car. You'll be asked to wear the rubber mask. Don't try to figure out where we are because you'll be wasting your time. You made the right decision today, Mr. Craig, and I'm sure your wife and kids would agree. By the way, they just went past our truck and turned on to River Road."

The dog walker put his weapon back into a shoulder holster and buttoned his suit jacket. "Meanwhile, for everyone's safety, keep your mouth shut. Jaime, move out with Mr. Craig in ten minutes. Give him his car keys now. Oh, and Mr. Craig, please take some of this Danish back with you to your office. We couldn't possibly eat all of it. Adios. I hope we don't have to meet again."

The dog walker put on his overcoat and hat, and then walked out of the room. Craig heard a front door open and close. Several men were still in the house watching him. He remained seated, waiting for Jaime to tell him when they were going to leave, hoping he could trust them to let him go.

Jaime was putting the remaining pastries into a box. He glanced at his watch. "Please put your coat back on. It's time to go."

Jaime carried the box of pastries out to the SUV where he helped Craig put on the full-face mask. He was put in the back seat and Jaime got in next to him. No one spoke on the return trip.

Twenty minutes later the SUV stopped and the driver got out and opened the left rear passenger door. Jaime told Craig to take off the rubber mask and sit still until his eyes adjusted to the daylight. Craig did what he was told, then was assisted out of the vehicle by the driver. Directly in front of the SUV sat his BMW.

The SUV driver said, "You drive away first. We will know when you get out onto River Road. Take care, Mr. Craig. Don't forget the Danish."

Craig got in his car and drove away. The SUV stayed there, with Jaime and the driver now both in the front seat. They did not move until Jaime got a cell phone call advising him that Craig was out on River Road heading toward Washington, DC.

# CHAPTER FOUR

R etired CIA Officer Nick Tarrant walked out of the coffee shop at 6:30 a.m. holding a large black Columbian coffee in his left hand and three newspapers in his right. His cell phone buzzed and he slipped the newspapers under his left arm before pulling out his phone from his leather jacket pocket.

"This better not be a marketing call," he muttered. He pressed the button to answer the call. "Hello?"

"Is this the oldest man in the world?"

Tarrant knew immediately the call was from his close friend and colleague Bill Slocum.

"No, this is the second oldest man in the world," he answered. "What can I do for you now that we are both out grazing in the retirement pasture? You in jail, or are a couple of outraged husbands sighting their hunting rifles on your house?"

Tarrant and Slocum's birthdays were only a day apart and they always ragged on each other about who was the oldest. Tarrant could tell by Slocum's tone this was not a casual call.

"Nick, we need to powwow," Slocum said in a serious voice. "It's going to be one of those days, as we used to say. I need to see you soon about something too hot to discuss on the phone, so get here *as soon* as you can."

"Full copy. How urgent? You know I hate rush-hour traffic, but if I wait some I could avoid the traffic and still be in your area by 10:30. And Bill, where are you, and where do you want to meet?"

"Meet me right here at the man cave and don't be late. We've got a problem. See you then. Out!"

Tarrant hated it, whenever over the years, Slocum said they had "a problem." Each time he uttered it, they indeed had a problem. Since both were retired from the Central Intelligence Agency after serving long careers, the new problem could be in any part of the world.

The man cave was a bungalow-sized building Slocum had built in his backyard next to the garage. He had everything in it: a full bath, twin beds, two large TVs on the wall, a dartboard, a sofa and two easy chairs, a card table, and a complete computer corner layout. There was also a large gun cabinet and bar. Bookcases lined two of the walls, and various memorabilia covered the other walls. It was a hideout with all the modern conveniences. It smelled clean and new.

Slocum had spent a lot of money on the man cave, money he had earned working on contract in the Middle East. The place was well heated in the winter and air conditioned in the summer. The only thing the man cave lacked was a full kitchen, though he had put in a microwave, a large liquor cabinet, a refrigerator, and two coffeemakers. Aside from his Dodge truck and a couple of old shotguns, the man cave was Bill Slocum's pride and joy.

Slocum was a large-framed former college athlete, an army vet with a tour in Vietnam, an established nonprofessional rugby player, a security guru, and an accomplished hunter and fisherman. He was a no-bullshit professional. With hands the size of a catcher's mitt, Slocum weighed easily around 270 pounds. As quickly as his persona could be intimidating, he also had great skills at making people feel at ease. He had an ability to make people think they were important and that he, Slocum, was listening to their every word. People came away from talking to him thinking that he was really trying to understand their point of view. He asked smart questions and was keenly aware of world events. He'd had a highly successful career at the CIA and had been a real friend of Tarrant's for years.

Nick Tarrant had been living in the Washington area for more than twenty years while pursuing his Agency career. Unfortunately for many, however, Tarrant was still, at the core of his being, a "Jersey guy." His Jersey accent was long gone but he still used Jersey neighborhood street vernacular and expletives, and still practiced survival skills learned growing up in tough, challenging neighborhoods where you treated people with respect and you helped out anyone down on their luck. You made friends and stood by people in times of need, and if you had to, you stood up and defended yourself. You did not have to win every fight; you only had to make it memorable. In Jersey, you could not be read as an easy mark.

If Tarrant thought someone was a stand-up guy, he wanted that person next to him when things began to go wobbly or worse, and he would repay the favor, if needed.

The two men had worked together for many years in the Agency and Tarrant knew Slocum to be a guy who would always give you the straight skinny, meaning the no-spin truth. On any number of occasions, Slocum had proven that he had Tarrant's back. He gave Tarrant good counsel and was fully discreet. Both were true CIA operational professionals who loved America. During their Agency careers they had witnessed too many deaths and injuries inflicted on special-operations officers when defending the country. Tarrant and Slocum were both troubled with what was going on today in America.

They were disturbed by the growing racial divisions, leftist and right-wing protesters brawling in the streets of Virginia and California, demands to take down historical civil war statues, restrictions and even denials for certain people to speak freely on university campuses, and repeated and unending examples of the government fumbling issues and mismanagement. The opioid epidemic especially bothered both of them because they had worked at different times with Drug Enforcement Agency officers trying to stop illegal drugs coming in from Asia and South America.

Tarrant recalled a conversation with a DEA officer who said, "For my entire career I have been shoveling sand against the tide. Each time I bust a drug trafficker, the cost of his competitors' product goes up. One trafficker who I was locking up looked at me and asked. 'When are you going to get it? It's all about market forces! Demand and supply.' He said you don't put traffickers out of business if the demand for the product is growing."

Tarrant thought the same point could be made today about the opioid epidemic. The demand was simply too great and Americans in both the inner cities and suburbs were killing themselves.

On many occasions, Tarrant and Slocum would be out drinking somewhere when they would start talking about what was in the news that day. Inevitably in the ensuing conversation they would ask each other why they seemed so out of touch with what was going on in America. Why were they apparently out of the loop, and how did it happen? Was it because they worked so many years overseas not to see what was eating at the values of their country? They never could find an answer but the conversation usually resulted in them ordering more drinks.

Tarrant's ride in from his house in West Virginia was easy, with traffic moving along without any real delays. Soon after retirement he had moved out of the Washington area to avoid such suffocating traffic problems. Congestion seemed to be growing worse. More bridges over the Potomac were needed, and the people who had to sit for hours in rush-hour traffic were growing more and more weary and angry. There was no relief in sight. It was wise for Tarrant to stagger travel times for car trips to very early, midmorning, midafternoon, or late-evening departure when he had to go into Washington. Any number of government employees were requesting permission to work out of their homes by telecommuting. It was easy to understand that their requests were about quality of life.

Tarrant never second-guessed his decision to get out of the immediate Washington area. His West Virginia home was very modern, extremely comfortable, and well protected by the most advanced security systems available. It had a shooting range, heated pool, Jacuzzi, several guest bedrooms, and a spacious first floor offering a dining room, a great room with a large fireplace, and a wonderfully enclosed back porch with bay windows. The kitchen was spectacular. The only complaint from visitors was that the ride out was too long. But those visitors loved the house and would often spend weekends at what they sometimes referred to as Fort Apache. Tarrant was an exceptional host.

Nick also had made friends with his neighbors and local police and firemen since moving to the country. He viewed them as an outer-defense perimeter. If needed, he was always there to assist them, and they would always be there for him. They counted on each other. They also knew he was retired from the CIA.

Nick pulled up in front of Slocum's house in Vienna, Virginia, a bit after 10:00 a.m. He saw his friend's truck pulled up near the garage and man cave. Nick got out of his three-year-old green Dodge Charger and started up the driveway. He had not gone ten yards when he looked over at the driveway next to Slocum's and saw a woman in a short skirt leaning into the trunk of her car getting out grocery bags. One large shopping bag was sitting on the ground and she was reaching in to get a second one. As she leaned in to get the bag, Nick took in her great legs and shapely butt. He simply stopped walking and stared as she lifted the bag out.

"Can I help you with those bags?" he called. "You must be Slocum's new neighbor."

She turned and smiled. She was even better looking from the front. She was stunning, with short brown hair, perfect teeth, a wide and engaging smile, and an overall great body. She was a knockout. Nick was clearly checking her out.

"Good morning," she said. "Yes, I'm the new neighbor. I only moved in a week ago. I appreciate your offer. I could use a hand to get these two bags up to my front door. You can take the heavy one because I almost couldn't budge it out of my car." She smiled and stepped out of Tarrant's way.

Tarrant happily picked up the second shopping bag and carried it up to the front door. "You want me to take it inside?" he offered.

"I have it from here," she said. "Thanks so much."

"It was my pleasure. I think you made my day. My name is Nick Tarrant, and I'm a good friend of Bill's."

"Hello, Nick. I'm Victoria Langeford." She took her hand off the shopping bag and reached out to shake his. Her handshake was strong and firm. "I just moved here from upstate New York. You can put the bag right here inside the front door." She pointed to the boxes piled all over the entry hall. "The place is still a mess from the move. Thanks again. I would have struggled with the bags."

"Victoria, it's a pleasure meeting you. I'm sure I'll see you again because Bill and I are old pals. Welcome to the neighborhood and have a great day."

As he was leaving he didn't turn around but instead was stepping out while still looking at her. What an attractive lady. He gave her a quick smile and wave and closed the front door. He crossed back over to Slocum's driveway and walked to the man cave where he banged on the door.

"Hold your horses, I'm coming." Slocum opened the door. "Did you take a bus to get here? I told you it was urgent. Get in here and grab a chair. You want coffee?"

Tarrant nodded.

"Milk and sugar in King Wuss's coffee?"

"Black works fine," Tarrant said, "but try to give me a clean cup. I just met your new neighbor and was very impressed. Is she single?"

Slocum shook his head. "Hey, buddy, slow down. I think I've seen you before in this movie at least a half dozen times. Yes, she is single. She is a new science professor at Northern Virginia College. And she is a nice neighbor who already has raked the leaves, walks her German shepherd three times a day, and seems comfortable driving her two-year-old Volvo."

Nick grinned. "If we had professors that good looking in my college science department, I would have majored in science. I would have probably flunked out in one semester because I would've been just sitting in class asking myself if I had any chance with her. She's a looker and seems nice. Again, I was very impressed."

They were now seated at the coffee table and Slocum put down his cup. His brow was knotted and his jaws clenched. "This is not about your now busted up and cratered love life, but more about the phone call I got last night from Doc Holliday."

Holliday was a career FBI agent who had worked with them on terrorist cases in the past. They shared trust and worked well together in spite of the history between the

FBI and CIA. Holliday was now a senior officer in the FBI's antiterrorism unit and, in Tarrant's world, a professional.

Slocum took a drink of coffee from a large mug. "Ed Pierce is dead. Murdered! Two bullets to the back of his head…a KGB-style execution knockdown."

Tarrant's eyes widened. "What? Where? When? Who took him out?" He sat back in his chair in shock.

The CIA's Directorate of Operations, or DO, was a special fraternity of professionals, men and women who made great sacrifices every day to help defend the country. A special bond existed between these officers.

Pierce had worked in the DO as a highly skilled reports officer for more than twenty years.

"Doc called late last night," Slocum said. "The night before, Ed was supposed to attend a retirement dinner party at his neighbor's house. The host thought it strange that Ed hadn't called to explain not showing up but covered for him and told the other guests Ed probably had some late-breaking issue at work. After dinner the neighbor still hadn't heard from Ed so he went over to his house and saw the car was in the driveway. The neighbor knew Ed was a stickler for detail and would have called if he had to cancel his plans. It wasn't that late so the neighbor rang the bell and knocked on the door. He got no response. He called Ed on his cell and got no response. The neighbor sensed something was wrong so he walked into the backyard and was going to knock on the back door when he saw light from the study. He thought Ed might be working on his computer and maybe had headphones on. He walked over to the window and looked in. Pierce was seated in a chair behind the desk in the study facing the window. His head was resting on the back of his chair with his eyes and mouth wide open. There appeared to be blood all over the back of the headrest of the chair. The neighbor ran back to the front of the house and called the police. By the time they got there the neighbor had called several others on the street and four neighbors were standing there when the cops arrived. Two of them were immediate next-door neighbors. They said they hadn't heard anything or seen anybody coming or going. All of them were upset and feared the worse.

"The police found the house fully locked up with no signs of breaking and entering. Nothing was out of place in the house and there were no signs of anything stolen. No signs of a struggle or any fingerprints found. The police investigators speculated that Pierce probably was talking to the killer or killers in his study when he was shot. They ruled out suicide and are officially dealing with it as a homicide. No weapon found, no gunpowder on Ed's hands to indicate he struggled for the gun, no bruises on his body. It was as clean a crime scene as you could ever find. The killer fired two .22 caliber rounds into the back of Pierce's head. The police are running forensics now to confirm it but they suspect the killer had a silencer on the pistol. The killers were real pros. The FBI thinks Pierce was probably looking at someone sitting in one of the chairs in front of the desk when the triggerman fired the two rounds into the back of his head."

Tarrant could not believe it. He and Pierce had become friends over the years. Pierce was a Middle East specialist, known as a strongly opinionated nonconformist. He was an outspoken subject-matter-expert (SME) analyst and reports officer on the region rather than the type of operations officer out recruiting and handling agent informants. One of Pierce's throwaway opening lines to the operatives was "What you guys don't understand is…" followed by whatever teaching point Pierce wanted to make. He was an expert on Iran and Saudi Arabia and he was highly respected by the operations officers.

"Doc told me he wants to meet with us off the record," Slocum said. "He knows we worked with Pierce and thinks we might know someone who had it in for him. He took me way off the record, saying there was something else he wanted to discuss with us. This something else is apparently a key part of an ongoing criminal investigation, so he says we are unofficially on notice to keep our mouths shut.

I told him we got the message. Loose lips sink ships. He said that was all good but if word ever got out that he was revealing these details to us he would be on thin ice with his FBI superiors."

Slocum put up a hand to rub his chin. "In Pierce's left front shirt pocket was a note wrapped around a ten of spades playing card. The note read, 'You need to learn from this.'"

"Who is the 'you' do you think?" Tarrant asked. "No addressee? And what's supposed to be learned?" Deep in thought, Tarrant got up and walked over for a refill of coffee.

When he sat back down, he said, "Okay, let's take this a step at a time. It was a professional hit…no clues, no witnesses, house locked with no signs of forced entry, and a message purposely left for the investigators to find along with a random playing card from a random deck of cards."

Tarrant took a drink of coffee. "What did Pierce do, or what was he up to before becoming a selected target? Doc obviously needs to comb through Ed's computer e-mails, bank records, insurance policies, phone records, and personal contacts. He's surely already doing all this so we don't tell a hunter how to hunt." Tarrant leaned back in his chair. "So Doc comes to us asking about any enemies Pierce might have had and whether we can make sense out of the message and playing card."

The two men then began to talk about their many memories of Pierce. He was a bachelor who seemed to enjoy the company of women. He was married to a Lebanese lady many years ago but that ended without animosity when she returned to Beirut to live with her aging parents. Based on what Pierce told Tarrant on one of their many trips together, Pierce and his wife had not had contact with each other for more than fifteen years. Slocum agreed with Tarrant that it would be a long shot to think his murder had anything to do with the wife or her family hiring a hit man to pay a call on Ed.

"What about the card?" Slocum asked. "Was Ed into gambling?"

"I've got to give the card more thought. For the many years I've known Ed Pierce, he never once mentioned gambling on anything. Doc may turn something over in Ed's e-mails or bank records to indicate he owed something to someone, but I'm drawing a blank about his ever being in any kind of debt. He was well known inside the intel community as outspoken about Sunni and Shia issues, and often took the side of the Shia and Iran against the Sunni and Saudi policies in the region. He shared Israeli concerns about Saudi fundamentalist Wahhabism, how it's being taught in schools all over Saudi Arabia and undercutting US influence and policy in the region."

Slocum nodded. "Maybe plain and simple it was a Saudi hit. Maybe they wanted to take out a policy critic and cut off his questions about Saudi contributions to terrorism via all that stuff about Wahhabi Islamic fundamentalist doctrine. Maybe his death was the message they wanted others to learn from. Perhaps the ten of spades was the triggerman's calling card left to prove he had carried out the contracted killing. This might be no more complicated than saying, 'Don't piss off the Saudis.'"

"But if it's the Saudis, I wonder why they suddenly needed to take drastic action now?" Tarrant posed. "Ed's position on Saudi policies hasn't changed for years and no one in policy-making circles has been giving his concerns more than a head nod. Wahhabism is on the policymakers' and politicians' to-do lists as something they'll address down the road, but the priority in the meantime has been to buy in on a partnership with Saudi Arabia to confront Iran.

"Besides, if the Saudis had decided to take Ed out, why would they kill him in his home? He traveled to the Middle East regularly. They could have arranged for him to be in a car accident, or the victim of a hold up gone bad in a marketplace, or a thief coming in at night to a hotel. Any of this could have happened on one of his trips and their tracks would have been covered. Why not simply kill him? Why raise suspicions by leaving a warning note?"

"What about the card?"

From his earliest years Tarrant had played cards regularly with his family and friends in New Jersey. Even as a kid, he was expected to know the games and play for nickels and dimes. He grew up playing cards. Card games were a centerpiece at family and neighborhood gatherings.

He took another sip of coffee. "A ten of spades in a regular card deck has no apparent meaning to me by itself. Did they find a deck of cards in the house missing the ten of spades? It could be a killer's calling card, just as you said. I've got to give the ten of spades a lot more thought. I wonder if it had something to do with his house, or neighbors, or something to do with work. I just don't know, but tell Doc we're putting our heads together and trying to assist. The more he can keep us plugged in to what the investigators are finding, the sooner we might be able to help him."

"Will do, but Doc said it's crucial to keep all of this off the radar because it's an ongoing criminal investigation, and it could be his ass if he's caught talking out of school," said Slocum.

"I read you, Lima Charlie. Mum's the word." Tarrant got up and walked toward the door. "I'll check a couple of rat lines with some of the old crew to find out if Ed was working on any new project or if there's been any recent issue that flared up and caused him trouble. See when Doc can meet us. Meanwhile, I'm a phone call away. Ed was a good guy and losing him is a bitch."

Tarrant walked slowly out to his car hoping for another chance meeting with the beautiful neighbor, but no such luck. It had been almost a year since his live-in girlfriend Anna had informed him she was leaving to go back to Israel. Months earlier Tarrant had sensed that they were growing apart. Anna had lived an exciting life before they got together and he sensed she was bored living outside of Washington, DC. She told him she missed her family and friends, and Tarrant never wanted to press too hard on exactly who were the friends, or friend, she was missing the most. He tried once to find out and she responded with a disarming smile, saying, "Ask me no questions and I'll tell you no lies." End of conversation. He acquiesced because he had his own list of off-the-table topics. They both knew it was over and Nick was not surprised when she left. They parted friends and in a sense would always respect each other. They'd had a special and happy relationship while it lasted and neither played the victim card when they parted.

The powerful Dodge Charger engine kicked off immediately after Nick turned on the ignition, with both four-barrel carburetors providing a low, throaty, and intim- idating sound. As he pulled away from the house, Nick envisioned the new neighbor leaning into the trunk of her car. He pictured her great legs and butt and then remembered the warmth of her smile and her good looks. How long had it been since Anna had left? He hadn't been out on a date since. Maybe it was time to get back into the guy-girl game.

When he arrived back at his house, he decided he was going to call Slocum and suggest that he put together a small dinner party and invite his new next-door neighbor.

# CHAPTER FIVE

S tephen Craig of the *Washington Gazette Bugle* was traumatized and outraged by his Monday morning "intervention." In the following days he had difficulty sleeping and keeping food down. He thought back on what happened and knew he'd never been more scared in his life, not only about his own safety but the safety of his family. Since then, when he looked at his wife and kids at dinner, he had mental flashes of the pickup truck starting to pass the car and then of the close-ups of the torn-apart bodies of the victims. Several times his wife or one of the kids had asked what was wrong but he'd deflected the query, saying he was just busy at work.

He tried to figure out what he could do about the situation. Should he go to anyone at the paper and tell them of the threat to him and his family? What could they do? Should he call the FBI, or one of his contacts in Washington Metropolitan Police? Should he call Ed Pierce? Should he talk with his wife and get her input? Was there any friend or mentor he could consult? There were negatives in each scenario and he just couldn't come up with a way to deal with this crisis without fear of putting himself or his family in greater danger. He remembered the quick, professional, almost rehearsed movements of those guys and their cold, threatening demeanor, and he knew they were not people you screwed around with.

Craig began to stagger his times going to work, often leaving later, after it was fully light, and finding some feeling of safety in the daylight. The more congested roads gave him a comforting sense that many people were around him, and there was safety in numbers. He would also go home early, after telling people at the paper he was writing a story at home and had to get going. He also found himself calling his wife several times during the day to be sure he knew where she was and to confirm she was all right. This did not go unnoticed.

One time she asked, "What's wrong, Stephen? Are you feeling okay? There seems to be something going on, and you're beginning to scare me. Talk to me! What's up?"

He deflected her concerns and questions by telling her he was working on a big story at the office that dealt with "tricky" issues. Fortunately, she did not press it and he offered no further explanation.

Every day for a week he mulled over his options only to decide in the end he was not going to open his mouth. He simply was too petrified in spite of every effort he made to remain steady and calm. Increasingly, he would close his office door, or sit alone at home, and turn all of this over in his head. He was agonizing over his decision.

He would not call Pierce and he would not tell anyone else what had happened. He told himself that to do nothing was the right decision and if he was ever challenged he'd deny he had given up a source's name, and anyone making such a claim would have to prove it. The guys who stopped him said they would not tell Pierce who gave them his name. Craig would take their word for it. He kept telling himself that they claimed they were only going to warn Pierce to stop leaking classified information. Such a conversation and warning wouldn't necessarily lead back to Craig or the *Gazette Bugle*. The people warning Pierce could have learned about him from any of a number of informants. Craig rationalized all of this by thinking that whomever these people were, they could have killed him. Instead they had only warned him. Surely they would do the same with Pierce. Craig hoped Pierce would agree to their demands to stop leaking classified information.

Craig was becoming a nervous wreck. He did not receive a call from Pierce. He also comforted himself that even if Pierce confronted him, he could explain the circumstances and Pierce would understand. Moreover, if his fellow journalists somehow later found out he had given up Pierce's name, they would understand his decision once they knew the pressure he'd been put under and the danger he and his family were facing. Once they knew the true story, they would certainly agree with his naming his source. He also believed they would understand his decision later to keep quiet and let the storm pass.

The more he turned it over in his mind, the more he felt the fourth estate would give him the benefit of the doubt and refrain from second-guessing his decision. Maybe he wouldn't be their hero as he was on three past occasions, but he'd certainly at least be cast as a victim in any of his subsequent discussions with those known to be the strongest advocates of freedom of the press.

The days passed, and Craig sat at his office desk, actually feeling himself falling into depression. He was having a terrible time concentrating. When his fellow workers and friends asked what was bothering him, he brushed their concerns off by hinting that he was working some things out at home. No one pressed him and increasingly they let him be alone with whatever problem he was having.

During this same period, Craig obsessed about Pierce, wondering whether he should call Pierce to warn him. The question was haunting him. If he did make the call, Craig knew he would have to take his family and go hide someplace. But where? Could the Feds and police protect all of them? And for how long? He would forever be looking over his shoulder. If these people ever did carry out their threat against one of his family members, how could he forgive himself?

At the end of each day, after the torment of asking himself what he should do, he decided there was too much to lose, so he'd better keep his mouth shut. Keeping quiet was the right decision. Yet none of this helped him sleep or eat any better, and his headaches were getting worse. The anxiety would begin the next day fresh and vigorous as the torment returned, and he once again tortured himself with questions about what he should do.

No matter what he tried to do to relieve the pressure—hot showers, chewing gum, smoking a cigar, taking a walk, listening to music—nothing seemed to work.

Things were not getting better and he began to feel he was getting sick. Those around him knew something strange was going on but they left him alone.

For a week and a half after his morning encounter with the dog walker, Craig told no one what had happened. He was an emotional wreck.

On a clear Thursday morning in his Washington office, Craig sat at his desk and looked blankly out the window. He was exhausted after another night of tossing and turning with very little sleep. He was feeling increasing pressure both at home and the office about what was troubling him. If they only knew!

He decided he needed to get some fresh air and told a secretary he was going out to get a coffee. He figured he could beat the morning crowd and get back to the office before the midmorning rush at the nearby Starbucks. He went in and ordered his coffee and was putting a lid on the cup at a side counter when a middle-aged man in an expensively tailored suit came up beside him.

"Hello, Mr. Craig. Let me have a word with you outside, please."

Craig had never seen this person before. The man walked out of the shop and positioned himself on the sidewalk across the street from the Starbucks's front door. He looked very fit. He probably was in his mid-forties with hair cut short on the sides and just beginning to turn gray. His arms were muscular and filled out the sleeves of the dark suit coat. His pant cuffs were tapered. Since he was not wearing a winter coat over his suit, Craig thought he must have just stepped out of one of the nearby office buildings to get coffee.

Craig had already put two sugars and a splash of cream into his Americano coffee. He put on the lid before buttoning his coat and stepping outside. The man was looking away from Craig as he approached. No one was in the vicinity of where the two men now stood and faced each other.

"I am a friend of those fellows who chatted you up a week and a half ago, and I'm here to give you an explanation of what you may soon hear, or perhaps have already heard."

Craig nervously looked around but no one was even remotely close enough to overhear their conversation. Two people entered Starbucks and one left, but no one was paying any attention to Craig and this stranger.

The man brought his cup of coffee up to his lips but did not take a drink. "Our…concerned citizens group met with Ed Pierce last night and tried to convince him of our point of view regarding leaking classified information," the man said. "Unfortunately, Ed was his usual argumentative self but even more belligerent than usual. He clearly was pissed off about our visit. He yammered on about how the

American public had a right to know the information he provided and told us in that arrogant voice of his that leaking classified information was as old as American baseball, so we all better get used to it. He said leaks are the way things are done today in Washington and that no one keeps secrets. He asked only once how we'd gotten his name but he never denied leaking the classified information."

The man looked directly into Craig's eyes as he took a drink of coffee. "Ed Pierce repeated that we better get used to leaking because that's the way things are done today here in the nation's capital."

Craig nodded to show he was listening, then asked, "Do you want me to talk to him?"

"No, Mr. Craig. Things went steadily downhill after he informed us for the third time that no one keeps secrets in the government today, so it's too late to talk any sense into him."

Craig gulped. "What do you mean?"

"I mean Ed Pierce has cashed in his chips. Mr. Pierce is gone."

Craig gasped and almost dropped his hot coffee. He felt he had been sucker punched. His body rocked back and forth.

"Take it easy, Mr. Craig, and pay attention to what I'm telling you. One, I want you to know we tried to talk to Mr. Pierce and convince him he was playing a dangerous game that had to stop. We could have killed him right after you had given us his name but we tried to talk sense into him."

Craig stood there wide-eyed and shuffling his feet, trying to deal with the shock of what he was hearing. It was unbelievable to listen to this man's low-key businesslike tone of voice about murdering a human being.

"Second, if you have told no one about your earlier conversation with us, you can rest assured no one will ever know you gave us Pierce's name. We'll keep that secret between us. Now that you know what happened, I think you know we don't like it when someone leaks secrets."

The man moved closer to Craig and was staring into his eyes. "That brings us to the third point, Mr. Craig. As of right now I want to remind you that you are out of the leaking secrets business. The next time you play the reckless game of gotcha with national security, you do so at your own risk. If we see you leak classified information again, we will take action. First against your family, and then you. The leaking game at the *Washington Gazette Bugle* is over for you, Mr. Craig. Do you have any questions?"

Craig moved his head side to side to indicate he had no questions. He couldn't have spoken if he had tried. His mouth was dry and his mind numb. Pierce was dead.

"My boss told me to tell you to go back into Starbucks and buy some Danish to take back to the office. He said a couple of your officemates really like Danish. Have a good day, Mr. Craig."

The man spun on his heel and quickly moved off in a fast, athletic walk. He rounded a corner and was out of sight before Craig's brain began to register what had just happened. The guy was scary. His clear eyes seemed to look right through him. His tone of voice was low key but threatening. Craig's bet was that this guy was a former special operator with the military or Agency. Whoever the man was, Craig's guess was that he knew a lot about killing.

Craig was shaken. His heart was pounding. He got back to his office and quickly found the *Gazette Bugle* already had a lead on a developing story about a CIA analyst by the name of Ed Pierce being murdered the night before. No details were available but the FBI was involved in the investigation.

He walked into his office in a daze, closed the door, and slumped into his chair. He recalled every word of the conversation with the stranger outside Starbucks. A note had been left on his desk while he was out that his editors had called an emergency meeting for the early afternoon. No subject was mentioned but Craig knew it was going to be about Ed Pierce. Craig's heart was still pounding and his stomach was turning over. He felt like he was walking on a beach in a Category 5 hurricane.

Feeling unsteady, he got up and told the office secretary he was going to take a sick day and go home. He told her he'd call the editors from there and reschedule a time to meet them. He next called his wife, saying he wasn't feeling well and was heading home. When he asked her if she had heard from the kids today, she started to ask, "Honey, is something wrong? What's wrong?" but Craig already had hung up.

# CHAPTER SIX

Slocum got through the security protocols at the front gate and drove down the long winding driveway to Tarrant's house. He parked his truck and got out. Tarrant was already standing on the front stone porch waiting for him. Slocum nodded up to his friend. As he approached, he looked around, trying to spot any new cameras or motion-sensing devices Tarrant had added to the security system around the house. Slocum couldn't spot any new equipment, but more than likely there had been an upgrade. Slocum was the first to brand his friend's residence Fort Apache.

"Hey, buddy," Tarrant said. "You are just in time for an early lunch. Come on in and relax. You made good time getting out here."

They shook hands and went into the house.

"You see the papers this morning?" Slocum asked.

"Yeah, I saw the Pierce story. They're carrying it as a homicide and hinting it may have been a break-and-entry robbery gone bad. No details and no mention in the newspapers of FBI involvement. Pierce is described as a government Middle East subject matter expert and author of several books about unrest in that area. So far they haven't mentioned Pierce worked for the Agency, but that's sure to come out. Did you hear back from Doc?"

Slocum nodded. "Spoke to him before I left to get out here. They're stymied. They're checking the locks to determine if there were any signs of tampering. All doors and windows were locked when the police got there. The intruders might have had a key or may have picked the locks. They're still dusting for fingerprints throughout the house and in his car, but so far have come up with nothing. Doc told me he thinks Pierce knew the visitors and let them in. They've confirmed the double-tap was from a .22 caliber with a silencer. There was absolutely no sign of a struggle or any indication that the body had been moved after he was shot." Slocum paused and took a deep breath. "I find it interesting that nothing apparently is missing in the house, with expensive TVs, stereo equipment, silverware, top-of-the-line computers and printers all sitting untouched and in place. They found Pierce's wallet with his license, credit cards, and insurance info all still in place. In the wallet there was also three hundred dollars in cash. The wallet was left untouched in Ed's back pocket.

"The forensics and crime scene team checked the computers and learned they hadn't been used for at least the previous thirty-eight hours. A check of phone records and his smart phone turned up nothing."

Slocum paused and looked at Tarrant while he let everything sink in. Tarrant was listening carefully and nodded.

"Doc said that Ed's neighbors noted nothing out of the ordinary the day before or night he was killed," Slocum went on. "No delivery trucks on the street or any repair being done at any of the nearby houses. All quiet. The mailman made his routine delivery late in the afternoon the day before Ed's body was found. When questioned, the mailman remembered dropping off mail to Pierce. This checked out when two credit card bills were found unopened on Pierce's desk in the study the next morning after the body was discovered."

Tarrant motioned Slocum to follow him into the dining room, where dishes and glasses were set out for lunch. They sat down and said nothing for at least a minute. Tarrant was factoring in all the information Slocum was giving him.

"Doc wants to meet us as soon as he can free up some time with all that's going on with the investigation. He reminded us for the second time to protect all this information. He confirmed your suspicion that there's no indication Pierce had any type of gambling problem or outstanding debt, so they're thinking the ten of spades is a dead end. He thinks the murder could be a terrorist hit and he needs our views on what Pierce was working on that might have made him a target. He even asked me if Mossad could've punched Pierce's ticket."

"The appearance of a double-tap execution with a .22 caliber pistol is more than likely what Doc's asking about when he surmises Mossad," Tarrant said. "But I think it's a real stretch to think Mossad paid the visit. Did he say anything else?"

"Pierce's finances were all in good shape. His friends are still being interviewed, but there's no hint of his ever being the least bit interested in gambling. What did turn up was Pierce's avid interest in theater. He was a regular patron of opening-night shows on Broadway stages and other New York theaters, and here in Washington. He kept this completely to himself inside the Agency but all his social friends knew about this interest and even on occasion joined him on a number of his trips to New York City for a premiere performance."

This was new to Tarrant. The door from the kitchen opened and Tarrant's trusted and able housekeeper, cook, and valued friend, minder, and employee, Consuela, carried in a large lunch tray with green salads, avocados, and chicken soup.

Consuela had worked for Tarrant for years after coming to the United States from Nicaragua, where she escaped from the Sandinista rulers. She had been singled out as a troublemaker and targeted in her small village when she spoke out against the Cubans directing the new Sandinista government. Her life was threatened and she was accused of being a Somoza supporter. She was detained and asked questions about contacts with Americans. Less than six months later, she left the country and crossed the border into El Salvador. Shortly thereafter she came to America. She'd received her US citizenship three years ago.

Truth be told, Consuela ran the Tarrant household. She shopped, cooked, cleaned, and served as the administrator for all of the house activities. She had Tarrant's complete confidence and trust. She fully understood Tarrant's rules about "need to know" and never pushed the boundaries. On any number of occasions, Tarrant called her and told her he had invited people to dinner that same night or houseguests were coming to stay with them. She would only ask how many and what time the meal was to be served. The guest rooms were always ready.

Tarrant described Consuela as a dream come true and viewed her now almost as a family member. He never took for granted her hard work, integrity, values, or friendship, because he did not want the dream ever to end.

Slocum and Consuela exchanged pleasantries, with Slocum as usual going out of his way to compliment her on the food selection, and telling her she was going to go directly to Heaven after working for "Señor Nick." He took the occasion to tell her Señor Nick was getting fat on all her good cooking.

Consuela laughed and served them their lunch. "Let me know if you want anything more," she said, and quietly left them alone to talk. The lunch was delicious.

A half hour later she opened the kitchen door and told Nick that unless he and Slocum wanted something else, she was going to go food shopping. Nick declined and said everything was good.

"Take your time shopping and come back and get some rest," he told her. Consuela said goodbye to Slocum and left.

"I've been giving the ten of spades playing card a lot of thought and want to bounce something off of you," Tarrant said. "I first started with the message 'We hope you will learn from this' and decided it was going to lead us nowhere. Who is the *we* and who is the *you* in the note? Was it left to confuse us and lead us off in the wrong direction? I guessed the lesson we were supposed to learn is that you don't do something Pierce did or you will be killed. But what did he do? I simply could not decipher the typed message, so I put it aside and focused on the playing card. Pierce did not play cards. No sign of a deck of cards found at the crime scene with the ten of spades missing. So the visitors came in with the card and left it as part of the warning message.

"I dismissed the gambling angle right from the start. His car was still in the driveway and not in some chop shop, and the visitors had his keys if they wanted to take the car. There was money still in his wallet, nothing valuable taken from the house, and apparently no sudden withdrawals from any bank account. If it was about him owing something on a large debt, he could have paid it off or the killers could have collected it in a number of ways before killing him. That's a rendition of the old refrain about not killing the *golden goose*."

Tarrant got up and invited Slocum to follow him into the great room, where they went over to the two large leather chairs sitting before the massive unlit fireplace.

"You want anything else to eat or drink? Maybe another beer?"

"No, I'm good," Slocum replied.

They sat down and Tarrant stretched out his legs. "I see the killer as a trained professional, whom you do not want to piss off. There are at least two of them, but I don't know if both are triggermen. They've shown me a lot already. These people don't leave clues behind, so right now we'd only be guessing at what happened. You can't take guesses into a courtroom. So for the last two days I haven't been thinking about who pulled the trigger or what the meaning of the typed message they left was. I've been thinking only about the ten of spades. Although it could be a reach, I've come up with an out-of-the-box scenario to bounce off of you, so hear me out."

"All right," Slocum agreed.

"The last time I could remember a playing card left on a body was in a special operation in Iraq. You'll recall that in some covert action and special ops that we've been involved in against terrorists, we've assigned values to high-interest targets."

Slocum nodded and leaned forward in his chair.

"We put together a deck of playing cards and assigned the top-dog terrorist the highest number and value, and gave smaller numbers to the others in the terrorist food chain. The top-dog terrorist was the ace in the deck. The second- and third-level leaders—the shooters, the bombers, couriers, bagmen, watch standers, and house sitters—

were all assigned less value because they were outriders or smaller fish. You'll remember in Iraq, US forces put pictures of these terrorists and their projected value amounts on playing cards to get the word out to the population that finding these terrorists would result in rewards. This was a rendition of the American Old West tactic of putting up wanted posters with a picture of the bad guy and a reward. Help take one of the bad guys down and you could collect this reward. It was a force multiplier and it kept the heat on the bad guys, who over time had to worry about trusting the people around them. Sow mistrust and increase the heat on the bad guy or target, give them more to worry about, and chip away at their safe havens. We tried to promote a game of 'Who can I trust?' for the terrorist leadership.

"So last night I'm sitting right here wondering if the ten of spades is part of a targeting strategy here in Washington. I asked myself who is the jack of spades, the queen, the king, and the ace? Is the queen a lady? Why could the ace not be a lady? So then I thought, okay, this is some sort of opening bid on a targeting strategy. Is there a royal flush out there somewhere? A royal flush is the highest hand in poker. Nothing beats it. A royal flush is the ten through ace of any one of the four suits in the deck of cards.

"So I reasoned that the ten of spades is part of a targeting strategy, the first card in building the royal flush. If so, there are four more targets out there. But even if I accepted the premise that this was part of a targeting strategy, I simply couldn't figure out how the killers expected the FBI to get their warning message out to others to stop doing what Pierce was doing. Whatever it was, it got him killed. I couldn't come up with an answer."

"So what do we do next?" asked Slocum.

"Ask Doc if there's been a playing card left at any other reported homicide in, say, the last two years. Also, ask if there has been any other homicide in the last two years involving a silenced .22 caliber pistol. Who was the victim? What was his occupation? Were any clues left at the crime scene? Was there any warning message left with the body? Is there any possible pattern in the playing card angle or use of a .22 caliber pistol to kill anyone else?"

"Got it," Slocum said. "I'll call Doc and see if we can get some answers."

Tarrant grinned. "By the way, see if you can get something back from Doc before Friday night."

Slocum nodded. "Why do we need answers before Friday night?"

"Because I'm going to attend a dinner party you didn't know you were planning to host at your house for some of your closest friends. You can order in some of that great Chinese food you live on during the week to avoid having to cook. And since you're going to be such a great host, be sure to invite your girlfriend, Karin, to attend. However, do nothing until you confirm your new neighbor can also stop over. If she is busy, try to pin down a date when she can come over. When you talk to that lady next door, tell her the guy who was recently admiring her out in her driveway will be there and is looking forward to seeing her again."

Slocum rolled his eyes. "I already told you, I've seen this movie a half dozen times. I'll do it only because I owe you any number of dinners, and come to think of it, I probably owe a couple of dinners to several others friends who have been feeding me out of the kindness of their hearts, knowing I don't cook. The fact I'll order in Chinese will make Karin's week. I'll call you by Wednesday noon."

Nick walked out with Slocum and down to his truck. "The ten of spades as part of a targeting strategy is me just thinking out loud. Let's keep it to ourselves until we get some answers back from Doc about any other playing cards at crime scenes, or any other double-tap murders with a silenced .22 caliber pistol. Oh, and don't forget about the dinner you want to host!"

Slocum got into his truck. "Yeah, yeah, you probably nodded off when I told you already I got it."

Tarrant tapped on the side of the door and Slocum rolled down the window. "Don't go ahead with planning the dinner if your next-door neighbor can't make it."

Slocum looked disgusted. "You're driving me nuts! I already told you I've seen this movie!"

★

Slocum called right on schedule Wednesday at noon and told Tarrant the dinner was on. He'd chatted with his neighbor who said, "Oh, him?" when Slocum told her Tarrant was coming to dinner. "She has a real sense of humor, because she asked if we were going to eat squirrel meat out of mess kits in the man cave." Slocum laughed. He also confirmed that Karin would be there. "She told me to tell you that you'd better be on your best behavior with the new neighbor."

Nothing appeared in any of the press about the Pierce homicide for the rest of the week. Nick told Consuela on Friday noon that he was going to Slocum's for dinner and might be arriving home late or even spending the night there.

He stopped to pick up wine and brandy on his way to Slocum's. He arrived at about 7:00 p.m. and parked in Slocum's driveway. The neighbor's car was in her driveway and her front porch and living room lights were on.

Tarrant knocked on Slocum's front door and heard the familiar growl.

"Hold your horses!" Slocum let Tarrant in and in a loud voice announced, "The oldest man in the world has arrived!"

Nick handed him the wine and brandy bottles and walked into the living room. Karin was standing with the new neighbor, Victoria, looking at one of Slocum's large oil paintings hanging between two full bookcases. The ladies were drinking wine and smiled when Nick approached and reached out to shake both their hands.

"Any trouble getting here?" Nick asked Victoria. "I could've picked you up."

While they smiled at each other, Karin said, "I was just suggesting I'd take her out tomorrow morning and drive her around to stores here in town and then out to Tyson's Corner. Next weekend we can do restaurants. After that I plan to brief her on dangerous men in the area she needs to avoid, men who have never grown up and still drive muscle cars." Karin looked at Tarrant and then over at Victoria and winked.

Tarrant laughed and lifted his glass of Irish whiskey. "You ladies look great tonight and it's a delight to be here with you."

Tarrant wasn't kidding. Victoria was wearing a short black dress and a string of white pearls. She was a real beauty. Who *was* this lady?

Slocum was holding a large glass of scotch on the rocks when he came up to the three of them. "Two other couples are also coming over. I've invited Tom and Judy Sullivan and Alice and Fred Whitaker. You'll like them, Victoria. They're great Americans and fun people."

The Sullivans were recently married after both being widowed for a number of years. Tom Sullivan was a retired polygraph expert and known to be one of the best in the business. He was a crackerjack at determining if people were telling the truth. He had been lied to by some of the best in the world of espionage, spying, and terrorism. His job was to not be fooled. His new wife had been a schoolteacher and highly interested in what was going on in national and world politics. She was quite a lady. Tom was a stand-up guy who had your back in a scrape. He was there when you needed him and you could be sure he would stand up with you to correct wrongdoing.

The Whitakers arrived shortly afterward. Alice was an attractive and creative interior decorator and quite busy in her private decorating business. Fred was a West Point graduate who, after he had left the army, later became a senior executive in the freight railroad business. Fred was a true patriot who loved the country he had sworn to defend. He felt there was no better country in the world than America. Fred was a smart guy who had been friends for years with both Slocum and Tarrant, and he was another member of the stand-up guy club.

Tarrant pulled Victoria aside and filled her in further on who the Sullivans and Whitakers were, and he assured her that she'd feel fully at ease with everyone there. He felt good standing close to her. He liked it that she tuned everything else out around her when he was talking. He went into some detail about Tom Sullivan's CIA background, saying that she better answer truthfully any of the questions he asked her tonight or he would call over Sullivan and get the truth out of her.

She smiled that great smile.

The dinner went smoothly and the food was delicious. They ate egg rolls followed by General Tso's lemon chicken, Yu-Shiang shrimp, Hunan beef, and both vegetable and Mandarin fried rice.

Everyone was fully engaged in friendly and fun conversations and seemed to be enjoying themselves. After dinner drinks were served, Victoria said to Nick, "Okay, you're all good friends but I thought CIA officers worked undercover and you weren't allowed to tell people what you did. How is it that Fred and Alice, and now I know you, Bill, and Tom, are all retired from the CIA?"

"I understand your confusion," Nick said, "and you're correct. Bill, Tom, and I have retired 'overtly' after getting the Agency's permission to come out from undercover. We don't talk about sources or methods or any out-of-bounds operational detail. We follow the 'need to know' dictum. But we now can tell people we worked for the Agency. Over long careers, our good friends already knew we were Agency."

Nick and Victoria looked up as Slocum walked to the center of the living room and lifted his glass to make a toast.

"Here's to our flag and to the men and women who have made and are making great sacrifices to defend it!"

Everyone lifted their glass and joined in the toast. From across the room Judy Sullivan asked Slocum if he was still watching NFL football games after the "kneel down" protests started.

"Nope, I'm watching very little of it. I'm no longer interested."

Tom Sullivan asked, "How about you, Nick?"

Slocum said in a loud voice, "Oh boy, battle stations!"

"I've got a real problem with disrespecting our flag," Nick said seriously, "and I think the players who are kneeling are sending the wrong message. But why ruin a wonderful evening with me getting on a high horse? Let's just say that the protesters could handle their issue better."

Nick grinned at Slocum, who had expected him to go off and run his mouth about the protesters taking a knee when the national anthem was played and the American flag raised. Only a week before in a bar in a downtown Washington hotel, Nick and a stuffy lawyer almost got into it about the NFL players kneeling. The lawyer, who quickly let it be known he had graduated from an Ivy League law school, argued that the protesters had the right under the Constitution to express themselves in that manner. Tarrant listened to him make his case and did not interrupt. The lawyer interpreted Tarrant's silence to mean that he was winning his argument.

After a while, Tarrant had asked, "You done, counselor?"

The lawyer picked up his drink. "I am."

Tarrant then asked the lawyer if he thought the owners of the football teams also had the right to bench the protesters because they were not representing the values of the owner, many of the players, or the fans. The lawyer would not concede it was the right of the owners to bench protesters who were protected under the constitution to voice their grievances by kneeling. Nick's questions about why the owners had no similar right to exercise their position only served to increase the intensity of the conversation. The lawyer then started to use the language about the "plantation mind-set" of the owners to heat things up even more. Both the lawyer and Tarrant were now off their seats and facing each other. At one point the lawyer told Nick he'd better watch his mouth because before getting his law degree he had played rugby in his college days.

Tarrant had smiled. "No shit! Really?"

Slocum finally stepped in between the two of them and they disengaged, agreeing they would disagree.

On their ride home Tarrant told Slocum that there were dozens of important burning issues out there in American society that needed to be addressed. Solutions might not be easy to find but things could get better if people better understood and discussed the issues without grandstanding. Tarrant, with his new oratory skills buttressed by his earlier drinking, said there was no priority order on any list about which issue was more important than the others. Slocum said nothing and just kept driving.

"Single out what you think are the five most important pressing issues facing US citizens today," Tarrant said, clearly wanting to have a discussion.

"What do you mean?"

"You know, what are the five things most Americans worry about today?"

Slocum did not respond.

"Let me help you," Tarrant said. "What do you think are the top five issues: poverty, cancer, crime, abortion, illegal immigration, taxes, deficit spending, discrimination, poor education, jobs, freedom of speech on campuses, religious freedom, police brutality, murder rates, Wall Street and government corruption, rising hospital premiums, Black Lives Matter, racism, failing transportation systems, low-income housing, illegal guns, nuclear attack, or opioids?"

Slocum said nothing for a couple of minutes.

"Well?" Tarrant prodded.

They drove in silence for another moment before Slocum said, "Could you repeat my choices?"

They both laughed, but that didn't end the discussion about the football players kneeling.

Nick said, "So in my way of thinking, if everyone knelt down because of one of these issues, we would raise the flag with everyone kneeling down. I'm suggesting that you don't disrespect the flag because you're fighting to resolve or make progress in solving one of these issues. Any one issue is not by decree the most important issue. They're all important."

When they got back to Slocum's house that night and were getting out of the truck, Nick said, "Of course, black lives matter, but protesters are now sending the wrong message by disrespecting the flag. There has to be a better way to address this issue. There is no better country than the USA. Do we have problems? Of course! But too many people have made the extreme sacrifice to defend our flag and country to let this go on. So I say, speak to the issues at hand without insulting the country we love and have fought to defend. There are too many stars on the CIA's wall memorial and too many grave markers in Arlington Cemetery to have Americans disrespect the flag."

The next morning Tarrant told Slocum that he was so worked up over the squabble with the lawyer that he hadn't slept well. Nick vowed he would avoid debating the issue in the future. Slocum only smiled and reminded Nick that he had once again saved his ass from a beatdown by an Ivy League rugby player.

"You mean beat down till I busted his nose or knocked him out?" Tarrant countered.

The dinner party guests did not know anything about Nick's confrontational debate with the lawyer or his strong feelings about the NFL protesters.

Slocum lifted his glass. "I applaud Nick for not really telling you how he feels, but I know what he's thinking. Here's to the new vicar of the congregation, Nick Tarrant, and to his insightful sermons, one of which he spared us all tonight. As I now remember his last sermon, may the next one please be shorter because I've got to go and piss. Hear, hear!"

Laughing, everyone their glasses and repeated, "Hear, hear!"

Nick glanced at Karin and said, "Tell him to be sure to use the bathroom and not to take a leak out front in the bushes."

As Slocum was heading for the bathroom, Fred Whitaker chimed in. "I was upset about the kneel down in London by the NFL protestors, after which they stood at attention for 'God Save the Queen.' That shows a real sense of understanding history, right? Give me a break! That London performance showed me a real ignorance about what people in this country know about world history."

Slocum was just getting near the bathroom door and in a loud door yelled back, "The NFL protesters in London can go piss up a rope!"

Glasses were lifted again.

The rest of the evening was relaxed and fun; there was no additional discussion about the NFL protest or any climbing on any other soapboxes.

"Do you want to stay the night?" Slocum asked Nick. When Nick agreed, he said, "Everything you need is already in the man cave," and gave him the key.

Before the dinner party broke up at about 11:00 p.m., Slocum whispered to Nick that Doc Holliday was supposed to call them in the morning.

The Sullivans left first, and then the Whitakers. Karin planned to stay the night with Slocum, and she began to help him clean up. Victoria volunteered to help but Slocum told her to go home and get a good night's sleep.

Tarrant said he would be staying the night in the man cave and offered to walk Victoria home. He thanked Slocum for an excellent dinner and told him he would see him in the morning.

Nick and Victoria got outside and the cool air was refreshing. They had enough streetlight to make navigating the trip across Slocum's lawn to her driveway and walkway easy.

When they reached her front door Nick said, "The only downside of tonight's dinner was that I didn't get a chance to hear you talk about yourself. I want to know who you are, what you like to do, where you want to go on this forced march called life. For all I know, a girl as beautiful as you may be soon engaged to be married, planning to enter a nunnery, or too busy chasing a career dream to have time to see someone."

"Maybe you want to call Sullivan back to hear my answers," she quipped. "How about we go in to my messy living room and have cognacs while we talk? You'll have to excuse the mess but I still have tons of boxes to unpack. Come to think of it, I have some questions about Mr. Nick Tarrant too, so maybe getting Tom Sullivan back here is not a bad idea."

They took off their coats in the hallway and she motioned for Nick to go into the living room where there were a number of unopened stacked boxes from the moving company. He sat down in an easy chair next to the sofa while she poured two cognacs.

"I'm giving you this refill only because I know you don't have to drive home tonight," Victoria said. "It was great to be with you and your friends at dinner. I really enjoyed it."

Nick had run too many agent meetings to miss this chance for her to talk about herself. He felt he was a lucky man to pull up and see her in the driveway. He had more great luck that she was Slocum's neighbor and would be living here for a good period of time. The more she answered his questions and talked about herself and her background, the luckier Tarrant felt. She was quite a young lady. That empty feeling he had since Anna left was now gone.

"Tell me about yourself," he said. "I want to know Victoria Langeford's likes and dislikes. I promise I'll answer any of your questions, but right now I want to hear about you."

★

Nick got into the man cave about 3:00 a.m. and immediately hit the sack. He began to dream of Victoria.

A little before 8 a.m. Nick walked into Slocum's kitchen. Slocum was in Bermuda shorts and a T-shirt in spite of the cooler weather and falling temperatures.

"How d'ja sleep?" Slocum asked when he saw Tarrant.

"Great, and the water in that man cave shower comes down like a tropical storm in the Darien jungle in Panama. It wakes you up fast. Did you hear anything from Holliday?"

Slocum was filling two coffee cups. "He said he'd call about ten. How'd your evening go with my new neighbor? Wait, don't tell me, I already know. She's now going to move out after experiencing your charm offensive."

Tarrant took his coffee cup from Slocum. "No, no…all good. She is a real classy lady but I must admit I was thinking of what it would have been like this morning if she had been under that shower with me in the man cave."

Holliday called right on time. No other crimes involving playing cards had turned up. There was only one case of a guy who had been bashed on the back of the head with a pipe and was doubled over on a table where he had been playing solitaire. Holliday added that there was nothing yet on the silenced .22 caliber angle, then asked if they'd come up with anything.

Slocum glanced at Tarrant while shrugging and lifting his brow. "Nothing new here, but we're working on it."

# CHAPTER SEVEN

For over eighteen years Dominic Pagelli had been an employee of the National Security Agency, or the NSA. When people asked him what exactly he did at his job, Pagelli would say he was a systems analyst, and then usually watch their eyes glaze over with disinterest. That suited him just fine because he was an important cog in the interwoven grinding mechanisms connected to Foreign Intelligence Surveillance Activities programs. These collection programs at FISA were aimed at court-authorized targets believed to be involved in or suspected of being connected to committing espionage in the United States. The court-authorized targets were viewed as endangering, in some form, US national security. Names of American citizens caught up in these collection efforts were supposedly protected under the citizens' constitutional rights and blocked out on FISA transcripts. But just as with many other government systems set up by bureaucrats and politicians, there were abuses, and on occasion, names of American citizens were leaked to the press. Of course, no names of the leakers were ever divulged because FISA activities were so highly classified. The leaks appeared to be politically motivated and made apparently to weaken or embarrass a political foe by hinting that the American citizen named might in some way be aiding a foreign power.

To date, no one in the FBI, CIA, NSA, Pentagon, office of the DNI, State Department, Justice, or White House had been found to be the source of the leak of an American's name. But the leaked name was right there in the press. The military's description of "fog of war" looked like a mild misty haze when compared with the density of thick cloud cover over the FISA procedures. The public got no answers, and the dangerous game of leaking FISA-related information went on. It seemed that on the surface of it, a political party targeted by the leak simply took note of the game being played and waited for the right time to return the favor to embarrass their political opponent. A rendition of the saying "What goes around, comes around."

Not one of the government's best investigative experts was able to locate the source of any leak of FISA information. This failure defied reason and led to the strong suspicion by many that it was clear political manipulation by the government in power to gain an advantage against a political enemy. Baseball fans knew that Washington politics was also a hardball sport, and during a regular season some batters do get hit in the head with fast balls. The names of American citizens involved in FISA coverage continued to appear in the press.

Although cast in the role of "I'll huff and I'll puff and blow your house down," nothing came out of Congress' feeble attempts to look into these leaks. One leaked story after another based on classified information appeared in the leading daily newspapers. Congress never found out who was providing the leaked information. They also ran into closed doors and dense fog when trying to talk about FISA information. Everything about FISA operations was highly classified. That is until someone leaked FISA information.

Dominic Pagelli grew up in Pittsburgh, Pennsylvania, the third son and youngest in a family-owned carpentry business. His father and uncle were master carpenters from the old school of craftsmen. They ran a successful shop and built it around repeat customers. Even in his early youth Dominic had been interested in technical things and played around with computers, calculators, cash registers, and repairing jukeboxes. In his early teenage years he developed an in-house audio system and installed it. Unfortunately, he was ordered to pull it out after he told his father he'd overheard his brothers talking in their bedroom about plans to egg and toilet paper a neighbor's house before Halloween. The neighbor was a teacher at the grammar school. Dominic's father came down hard on all the boys, but hardest on Dominic, who his father explained had broken a rule when he ratted out his brothers. He said Dominic should have gone to his brothers and told them he would tell their father only if they went ahead with their plan. Dominic thought it was easy for his father to say that, but he was going to get the bruises from his brothers.

Dominic had graduated with honors from MIT in 1999 and took a summer vacation in Europe after graduation. The next fall he'd interviewed with NSA and was hired. He moved up the NSA promotion ladder quickly thereafter and was enjoying a distinguished career. He liked the fact that he never had to tell anyone what he was doing at work. In 2016, he began to work on FISA issues.

He never married and seemed to be too much of a "techy" type and loner to interest any girls wanting to have a long-term relationship with him. He wasn't bothered by these rejections and was quite content to live in his own tech-world bubble. He'd moved into a nice house in an upscale Maryland neighborhood in 2010 and soon built solid friendships and social relationships with neighbors. On weekends he usually would be found helping one of them out with a computer problem or in his favorite pastime of cooking. Over time he began throwing small dinner parties for his neighbors to try out one of his new recipes. Soon they began returning the favor. His neighborhood guests were highly educated, well-read, and successful people. There were government officials from the usual alphabet soup of agencies and departments. Others were fashion designers, lawyers, real estate agents, construction engineers, and supervisors. There were also two aspiring writers and a leading journalist from the *Washington Gazette Bugle*. This last person, an attractive middle-aged divorcee, lived at the end of his street. She jogged every other day and did yoga four times a week. She was fond of Dominic Pagelli and frequently would socialize with him on the dinner circuit, or when she called him over to her house to fix a computer problem. She did a lot of *Gazette Bugle* work on her computer from home. Whether or not it was computer glitches or sharing cooking recipes, she and Dominic were spending more and more time together.

Dominic was enjoying his life living in the tranquility in the outskirts of Laurel, Maryland. He had time to read and relax, and to do the cooking he loved.

He felt like he was living the American Dream, and all of it without the sound of anyone driving nails into pieces of wood, the racket and noise of wood sanders, or electric saws, or people in the background yelling.

Dominic Pagelli was content and satisfied…a state of mind that would soon change.

# CHAPTER EIGHT

The Laurel Police Department got the call at 9:00 a.m. on a Friday morning and responded immediately. The two policemen in the squad car pulled up and saw two elderly women standing outside the front of the house on the quiet and peaceful suburban street. A car was parked in the driveway. As they were getting out of their car, one of the women came up to the police officers.

"I'm the one who called you." She was nervous and upset. She said she'd suspected something was wrong at her neighbor's house. "My neighbor always leaves for work at six a.m. Monday through Friday. You can set your watch by his departure. When I looked out my kitchen window earlier today, at seven-thirty a.m., I saw his car was still there. An hour later I went out to pick up my newspaper and the car had not moved. I went over and knocked on his door and rang the bell, but got no response. I was scared maybe he had fallen or had a heart attack."

By then, the second woman, her neighbor from across the street, had joined her and suggested they go together and knock on the side door of the house, which they had done. There was no response. Concerned, they looked through the small windows framing the front door. They could see their neighbor's attaché case in the hallway, so they rang the bell before trying to call him on the next-door neighbor's cell phone. They tried his phone again, and then a third time before calling the police.

"Please remain calm," the sergeant said. "My partner and I will take a look. Please wait out near the front side-walk while we check on the homeowner."

The two policemen went up to the front door and tried the bell. The sergeant banged hard on the front door with his fist before taking off his flashlight from his belt and banging louder on the door. The other policeman went down to the side door and knocked loudly. Both policemen calling, "Hello, hello, Mr. Pagelli, can you hear us?"

The sergeant radioed and asked dispatch to send an EMS unit to the address. Once he heard back from dispatch that EMS was on the way, he'd told his partner he would go down in the backyard to see if Mr. Pagelli might hear him knocking or calling from there. He told his partner to wait at the front door and look in through the small windows on the door to see if there was any sign of Mr. Pagelli. Several minutes later the sergeant came back saying he had gotten no response.

The EMS unit rolled into the driveway and stopped behind the owner's parked car. Both policemen turned on their body cams. The sergeant made one last attempt to bang on the door with his flashlight before busting a small pane of glass on the doorframe and putting his hand in to unlock the front door.

"Mr. Pagelli, are you here?" he yelled into the house. "Mr. Pagelli?"

The two EMS responders stood outside near the front of the owner's parked car but did not enter. The two Good Samaritan neighbors stood even farther away, nervously watching.

As the sergeant went down the hallway toward the entrance to the kitchen, he saw a body lying face down with a pool of blood spreading out under the person's head. He immediately drew his weapon and called in to dispatch to report a homicide. His partner drew his weapon and took up a defensive position to protect his partner's back. The killer could still be in the house.

Backup police units responded quickly, and soon six policemen were searching the house. Two of the policemen who had just arrived checked the victim's pulse. After an all-clear was announced for the dwelling, the sergeant called in the EMS techs to come in and check the victim. The sergeant was holding out hope that the man might have a chance to survive.

The police captain who had responded to the call joined them and looked at the body. He shook his head. "The victim more than likely was dead before he hit the floor."

The two elderly ladies were given no details of what the police found but were asked to go back to their houses and told that the police would come over soon to talk with them. They kept asking what had happened. Had he fallen? Had he had a heart attack? Where was Mr. Pagelli? What was going on?

The Pagelli house was sealed off as a crime scene. Other neighbors had now come out of their homes on the street to find out what the commotion was all about. The coroner was called and a sense of shock quickly set in on the sleepy, upscale street in suburban Maryland.

From a distance, and certainly from early indications, it appeared this incident would be just another entry on the weekly police blotter, but it quickly became a story on the local evening news.

# CHAPTER NINE

**D**oc Holliday called Slocum about noon on Friday and told him that he urgently needed to see both Slocum and Tarrant that same night. He gave no details. Tarrant got the relay call from Slocum and set out immediately for downtown DC.

At 8:30 p.m. Tarrant and Slocum walked into Donley's Pub where they were to meet Doc Holliday.

It never failed to impress Tarrant what happened when he and Slocum walked into a bar or nightclub. Patrons would look at Slocum's size and ask themselves, *Who is this guy, and who's he looking for?* By the looks on their faces, they probably also were figuring there was going to be trouble. Tarrant would come in only a few moments after, just steps behind Slocum, and no one would notice him. Tarrant joked that he could have a parrot on his shoulder, be wearing an eye patch, and have a puppet on one hand and he would not be noticed. When Tarrant told this story he always ended it by saying it was good to go around with big, ugly friends.

Holliday was already in the pub, sitting on a stool at the far end of the bar with no one near him. Lights were dim and it looked like a good place to talk. At the other end of the bar were two patrons sitting on stools watching a sports-junkie show on a large wall-mounted TV. The whole place was dark. The deep brown wooden panels on the walls seemed to make it darker.

The bartender nodded to both Tarrant and Slocum and then brought down their usual one Irish whiskey and a Kentucky bourbon. He asked Holliday if he was ready for a refill but Holliday declined. The bartender walked back to watch the sports program.

Holliday lifted his glass in a toast. "Here's to the good guys and piss on the bad guys."

"Good to see you, Doc," Nick said after their toast, then cut to the chase. "Something big must be up."

"We've got another homicide and this time with a jack of spades left on the body along with another double-tap to the head with a silenced .22 caliber. The playing card was wrapped in a note. This one stating, 'Some folks are simply not getting the message to cease and desist.'"

Holliday provided details of the killing. The victim was a career officer at NSA, no clues left behind in the house. All the doors were locked, no fingerprints. Nothing appeared to be stolen, car and car keys still there, nothing found on computers, no deck of playing cards. Neighbors had heard nothing. An absolutely clean crime scene.

Although neither Tarrant nor Slocum had ever crossed paths with Pagelli, they listened carefully as Holliday filled them in on who the victim was, where he was working, and in general terms what he was working on. A full investigation was underway but these killers were clearly showing they were real pros. They did not leave loose ends.

"The lab confirmed that the ten and jack of spades came from the same deck of playing cards," Holliday said. "No sign of forced entry. This time the note was left between the victim's splayed legs and away from the pool of blood under his head. There was no sign of a struggle and the victim was probably killed as he started to walk down the hallway. The body had not been moved."

Tarrant shook his head, taking it all in. "Tell us more about the victim. Did he have any gambling connections? Was he in debt to anyone? Any idea of what he was doing to have not understood the apparent order of the day to cease and desist?"

Doc took another sip of his drink. "Nothing so far. This guy was living the dream. He had a very successful career. He had a small mortgage outstanding on his house and recently paid cash for a new car. He was a bachelor and had a lot of neighborhood friends, no issue of guy-guy or girl-guy problems, no known threats against him. He appeared to be a model citizen. He recently got back from a TDY in Afghanistan on some kind of hush-hush intercept program but his usual work at NSA was as a highly ranked official on FISA issues."

Doc called the bartender down to set up another round of drinks and waited until the bartender went back to the TV before he went on. "NSA keeps a careful watch on its employees. Pagelli had no workplace issues, no prostitutes, no drugs, no sex issues about any jilted lover, no debts, nothing. Nothing but a double-tap and a warning note wrapped around a playing card."

"Okay, let's agree that these guys are real professionals," Tarrant said. "Obviously, Pagelli and Pierce have to be connected in some way."

Doc nodded. "We're checking to see if they were members of the same club, a church, a school, anything like that. And we're trying to determine if they had a mutual friend who could be the connection. We're trying to do the old connect the dots but getting nowhere. Whatever they were doing, somebody wanted them to stop doing it. We're also checking to see if either was involved in any sort of a commercial deal or investment that went bust or maybe they backed out from. Whatever it was, it had to be for high stakes because it got them both killed.

"The pistol had a silencer on it. Forensics confirmed it was the same murder weapon. The shooter was standing behind the victim when he pulled the trigger, like with Pierce. Pagelli appeared to have been walking out to gather his things from the table in the hallway on his way out the front door. They have no idea if he was talking to anyone in front of him when he was shot."

They reviewed the details Holliday had given them about the crime scene before talking about the message and playing card.

Tarrant explained to Holliday that he and Slocum thought the meaning of leaving the playing cards on the bodies was possibly part of a targeting strategy. "I don't know for certain the meaning of the playing cards but it's worth thinking about."

Tarrant then reviewed how cards were used in the past in operations targeting terrorists, and most recently used in Iraq. "It was a rendition of the Old West wanted posters that placed a financial reward on the heads of the outlaws. The ten and jack of spades are part of the poker royal flush, and therefore at least three more targets are out there to complete the royal flush. The challenge facing the FBI is to get the word out to whomever the other targets are. But who they are is a mystery, so the mission is to find the killers and stop them before they kill again."

"I'll give all of that extra thought," Doc said. "In the meantime we're working with NSA to determine if anything Pagelli was doing at work could have caused him to be killed. I've got to be real careful here because of secrecy laws surrounding FISA. Another angle we're working on is his hobby of cooking. He was an aspiring cook and an amateur chef with a social life centered around cooking, hosting, and attending quiet private dinners. Most of the social activity took place in his suburban neighborhood and we're now interviewing those who participated in these regularly scheduled events."

"Did he have any foreign contacts?" Slocum asked. "Could he have been recruited and working for a foreign intelligence service? And what was he doing on his last TDY out to Afghanistan? Did he cross wires out there with anyone in illegal drug trafficking?"

"All good questions," Doc said. "FBI investigators are working to get some answers."

Nick said, "Okay, let's do a hot wash. We have two murder victims who were killed by the same professional killers. They left a warning note on each target, along with a playing card from the same deck. We are combing through each man's personal and professional history to find any kind of a connection between them. The warning messages imply both victims were breaking a rule or an agreement. Did the victims make a deal and then back out? Who are the killers warning when they tell others not make the same mistakes? The phrase 'cease and desist' means both Pierce and Pagelli had to be doing something that cost them their lives. Look, Doc, let's meet after you do the scrub on Pagelli's workplace and list of friends. We need to know if any of his crowd knew Pierce. Is anyone in Pagelli's circle of friends and fellow workers related to Pierce? We've got to find out more information if we are ever going to figure this out."

On the ride back to Slocum's, Tarrant remained silent and deep in thought.

"What's up, Lone Ranger?" Slocum asked.

"I'm giving the playing cards a lot of thought. You heard me tell Doc that the ten and jack of spades are two of the five cards in a royal flush, which means, if I'm right, there are three other targets out there to complete the royal flush. The next card would be the queen, and I'm wondering if this means the next target could be a female. They're sending warnings to the next three targets to cease and desist, but what the hell were the two victims doing that the killers want to stop? I'm convinced the playing cards are from a page out of special operations. I'm thinking the killers might be black-ops guys playing off the reservation. Or they could be operators still on the reservation and working in government. But why the hell are they so pissed off?"

Tarrant stayed the night at Slocum's, but before going to bed he called Victoria and asked if she had time the next morning to have breakfast with him at the Silver Diner in Tyson's Corner. She said she had a class at 10:30 a.m. but could meet him at eight for a quick breakfast and still be on time for the class. She said she knew where the diner was located and would see him there.

Tarrant left early the next morning. Victoria's car was still in her driveway. He went out to recon the diner area, proving old street operators' trade craft habits die hard. He spotted no surveillance outside the diner or inside, but why would there be?

She walked into the Silver Diner right at 8:00 a.m. and Tarrant motioned her over to a booth. She looked great in her blue skirt, white blouse, stockings, and short form-fitting winter coat. Nick looked her up and down and smiled. He wondered how many of her college students would be having a hard time paying attention today during her lectures.

"Any trouble getting here? I saw your car in the driveway when I left Slocum's and wondered if I should wait for you just to be sure you knew the way to the diner."

"No problem at all. I stopped off here once or twice in the last week to get a coffee to take with me on my drive to school. I didn't know you were at Slocum's last night. You should have told me and I could have prepared some breakfast at my place."

Tarrant smiled. "Thanks, but I didn't want to give you something else to do during a workweek."

They ordered breakfast. Victoria asked for a short stack of blueberry pancakes and Tarrant ordered his usual two eggs sunny side, bacon, and an English muffin.

"Were you guys out last night shutting down one of your watering holes or are you working on something?" Victoria asked. "Bill Slocum told me at times you both do consulting work."

"I only wish we were out enjoying ourselves," Tarrant replied ruefully. "No, we were out putting our heads together trying to figure out who is behind a crime."

Her eyes opened wider. "What do you mean 'a crime'? Something happened in our neighborhood? Was it near my house? Do I need to get more locks and lighting? Am I safe walking my dog? Should I—"

Tarrant reached across the table and put his hand over her folded hands. "Relax, it has nothing to do with your neighborhood, and it's not a robbery. It's a homicide. We're trying to help a friend who is a criminal investigator. He's picking our brains on who could've done it. He hasn't ruled out terrorism or international intrigue, so he wants to get our input."

She was relieved and looked interested in hearing more.

"Whomever it is we're dealing with, it's clear they're real pros," Tarrant said. "They know exactly what they're doing and they leave absolutely no clues or traces behind. We're trying to connect the dots but we're not off to a good start."

"Sounds interesting," she said, pouring more coffee into their cups from the carafe the waitress had left. "I'm an avid reader of detective novels and one of my heroes is the infamous Jack Reacher. Your story sounds like a plot in a Jack Reacher book."

Nick smiled. "Slocum and I could use Jack Reacher right about now. Oh, before I forget, I want to ask if you could come out to dinner at my place on Saturday night. You could ride out with Slocum and Karin because it's a bit of a haul to get there. This time of the year we have deer on the roads. That changes after hunting season kicks in, but even then you've got to be careful a deer doesn't run out in front of you. Dress code is informal. The folks you met at Slocum's will all be there and I promise I won't say another word about football. I'd like it if you could come out."

"Nick, I'm glad we met," Victoria said. "Our discussion the other night was so enjoyable. I had been so fixated on the move, unpacking, settling in to the new house, and adjusting to the new job, that I was beginning to think it was all a big mistake and I should have stayed in New York. You listened to me and it helped me put a lot of these things in perspective. I felt good afterward that I had gotten all issues out on the table."

She smiled and squeezed his hand. "Count me in for the weekend, but how about me reciprocating with a dinner at my place the following week? I need to find out if the oven and electric range work and it'll give me a reason to get my dishes out of the boxes and washed."

Nick nodded. "You're on, but the word reciprocate scares me. If you don't like the food I serve, you'll try to get even with me. That means I might have two bad meals instead of one."

She grinned at him, then looked at her wristwatch. "Oh, brother, look at the time. I've got to skedaddle. Thanks for breakfast and let's talk during the week. Think about what I can bring with me for your dinner on Saturday."

"You just getting there is more than enough, but bring a big appetite. I'll call Slocum and tell him you're coming out to my place with them. What's the best time to call you during the week?"

"You can call any time after eight p.m." Victoria thanked him for breakfast again and he watched her walk out. She had his full attention.

She was striking. He wondered if it was too late for him to take a college science course.

On the ride back to his house, Tarrant kept trying to connect the dots in the two murders and finally gave up. He started to think about seeing Victoria again, but quickly thought that he'd better get his mind back on driving safely and not thinking about her body, her lips, her great looks and personality. She was the whole package, beauty *and* brains.

To distract himself, he started playing surveillance games, first searching for any possible surveillance on him and then playing the role of being a surveillant by choosing a vehicle somewhere ahead of him to follow. If the vehicle turned off, Nick would simply choose another target. He practiced being three or four car lengths back and then moving up to the first and second slots. Time seemed to go by faster with these mind games and soon he was home.

He went into the house and informed Consuela that they had an important dinner coming up on Saturday night and she should pull out all the stops to make it a success. He asked that she prepare his favorite *lomo saltado*, the dish he had loved since his days in Lima.

Consuela asked how many were coming for dinner and surmised there had to be a new special lady guest invited given Tarrant's enthusiasm. She also suggested they might want to change the menu. He had not entertained a lady friend at the house since Anna had departed, and Nick was now asking her to be sure this Saturday night dinner was a great success. She was glad for Nick. It was about time.

★

By midweek Doc Holliday had already called twice with updates. The FBI interviews of friends and relatives of the two victims continued, and as yet there was simply no hint of any connection between the two men killed. They were still pulling their hair out. Doc said they were drilling deeper and knew they had to get answers before there was a third killing.

Tarrant spent the rest of the week seeking out and talking privately with some of the old network of special operators, including from the Agency, the Pentagon, the military's Tier One strike forces, police, and private Beltway bandit security firms. He asked if anyone knew Pierce or Pagelli, or if they had heard of any markers out on either man because of something they had done or failed to do. He asked his contacts if they had heard anything about the killings and what might have royally pissed off the killers. Then he talked about the .22 caliber double-tap to the back of the head, asking if any of them had heard anything about anyone ordering such executions. On several occasions, when talking with only his most trusted special-operator friends, he stepped across the line and asked if they knew of any black-ops warrior who left such a targeting card on a body. All his contacts agreed to put their ears to the ground and listen for anything out there that might be going on. Nick assured them that any information they provided would be protected and their names not brought into discussions. He ended each private chat with an urgent plea for their help in avoiding a third killing.

After checking his trusted "rat lines" into the special-ops world, he contacted Doc Holliday to say that none of his contacts thought it was terrorists. Several of them had gone into gruesome detail as to what would have happened to the targets if terrorists from the sandbox had taken them out. The killings would have been videotaped, the targets would have been pleading for their lives, and the throats of both men would have been slashed open while the camera was doing a close-up of the target's eyes wide open and the blood gurgling up from their cut-open throats. The killers would have been wearing masks and there would have been a statement read or recited by the executioner about the errors the targets had made.

"I'm satisfied that I've now set up a system of trip wires to warn me if one of the special operators has gone rogue," Tarrant concluded. "My contacts have their ears to the ground and will pick up any rumors out there."

# CHAPTER TEN

Steven Craig was assigned to room 418 in the North West Washington Health and Rehabilitation Center. He had been in there for two weeks, ever since the terrifying night in the emergency room at Sibley Hospital. Craig had had a stroke, and by this time had been out of his office for almost three weeks. In the days leading up to the stroke, his fellow workers, friends, and family members thought he was acting strangely. His colleagues had thought something was going on at home and hadn't wanted to pry. His family members thought something was weighing on his mind from work and that explained why he was becoming less and less communicative. Behind his back, several people in his office feared Craig was falling into depression. No one took any action for fear that Craig would regard them as interfering.

One morning at work while he was reviewing a draft, Craig collapsed and was rushed to the hospital. It was obvious he had had a stroke and he was put on breathing and feeding tubes. He was left partially paralyzed on his right side. His speech was impaired and doctors cautioned that he might have suffered extensive brain damage.

In the first week after his stroke, he did not recognize his wife or kids and did not seem to be focusing his eyes on anyone in the room. No one knew if he could hear them and visitors could not understand any of his verbal responses.

His wife could not explain what had happened but was aware that something was troubling her husband in the weeks right before he collapsed. When the doctor asked her what exactly she meant, she said something seemed to be upsetting him and he clearly was not himself. She had attempted on several occasions to get him to talk about what was going on, but he had ignored her pleas.

His regular doctor told his wife there had been no warning sign in his last annual medical examination to indicate he was in any danger of having a stroke. The doctor expressed regret that his patient had not contacted him in the weeks before the stroke when he apparently was growing more and more depressed. The doctor asked his wife to check with the newspaper staff to find out if there was something at work that was dragging him down and not letting him sleep or eat.

He pointed out that Craig did not have a regular physical fitness regimen, ate meals on the run, and had an irregular sleep schedule. He had all the "poster boy" symptoms of the man blindly chasing his career goals and ignoring common sense health guidelines. He shook his head, saying that too many people ignored these guidelines until it was too late.

The doctors at the treatment center told the family that all stroke patients suffer some permanent damage, but they had to wait and see exactly what the long-term effects would be on Mr. Craig. Craig sat in a wheelchair next to his wife in the center's all-purpose room, showing no indication that he understood a word of what was being said around him. His wife's eyes filled with tears and the doctor patted her on the shoulder to indicate he knew what she was feeling.

Every afternoon thereafter at the same time, a health technician would wheel Craig out to the all-purpose room just to break the monotony of sitting in his small hospital room. He'd wheel him over to an area in front of one of the many large windows and position the wheelchair to allow

Craig to look out onto the grounds and see the changing colors of the leaves still on the trees. The technician wanted to get him out of his room but also to let him hear and see other people. The only response from Craig was that he periodically would roll his head from side to side or move his shoulders up and down. An almost full recovery from a stroke was not unheard of, but Craig clearly had a long struggle ahead of him.

His verbal responses were still difficult to understand, but one positive sign was that he now was able to focus on someone who was talking to him.

# CHAPTER ELEVEN

T arrant's dinner on Saturday night went extremely well. The guests, as expected, were relaxed and engaging. All were friends, and the topics of conversation ranged from national and international politics to great shopping buys for the upcoming holidays. There was not one mention of sports.

Victoria was awed by the size and beauty of Tarrant's house and the state-of-the-art security system that protected it with cameras, lights, and alarms. As the dinner guests arrived, greeted each other, and kibitzed, Tarrant took her by the arm and walked her around the house. He introduced her to Consuela and told her Consuela was the brains of the outfit. Consuela showed real interest in Victoria and seemed to be the fully focused hostess, not the multitasking cook.

Consuela told her about Nick and how long they had been together. The ladies agreed to have a more detailed chat at another time and maybe share recipes. Victoria looked about the kitchen, and seeing all that was going on politely excused herself, telling Consuela she looked forward to seeing her again. What struck Victoria was that Consuela made her feel their short talk was the only thing important at that moment. She made Victoria feel very welcomed.

Before dinner Nick showed her the upstairs with the bedrooms, baths, and reading room with the various camera feeds from the outside security systems.

"Why do you have such an extensive camera system?" she asked.

"It's a carryover from living so many years overseas in dangerous countries where Americans are targets," he replied.

The food was outstanding and the conversation enjoyable. Consuela had indeed changed the menu. Shrimp cocktails and green salads were followed by roast beef, baked potatoes and gravy, and asparagus. Afterward, chocolate layer cake was served with tea and coffee. There was a lot of discussion about the "hidden hand" of the Cubans in supporting the Venezuelan dictator Maduro and how this had been ignored by the United States when reopening relations with Cuba. This led quickly to more discussion about the remaining Russian influence in Cuba and its impact on Cuban policy toward the United States.

For the most part Tarrant only listened as his guests discussed these various topics. He was in the role of the genial host and was there to assure they all had their glasses filled and seconds on the food. From time to time he would lean over and ask Victoria how she was doing and whether she was enjoying herself. The Sullivans and Whitakers also went out of their way to ask Victoria how her week had gone and if she was having any problems settling in.

Slocum and Tarrant seemed relaxed. They periodically asked a question or added a comment to indicate they had not missed a bit of the ongoing conversation. Even though both men's minds were preoccupied with Pierce and Pagelli, they were trained operations officers who were accustomed to handling stress.

After dinner, the guests went into the great room where Nick served cognac and brandy.

At 10:30 p.m. Karin told Slocum that she needed to get back home since she was helping put on a church breakfast the next morning and would have to be up early. Slocum asked Victoria if she was ready to move out and she said yes.

Slocum looked at Tarrant as if he expected Nick to make a play for Victoria to stay the night.

Instead, Nick said, "Victoria, you made my evening by being here. I'll call you tomorrow. You didn't even have seconds on the food so I've got to report you to Consuela. Please note for the record that Slocum had thirds."

The other guests followed suit and began gathering their things to go home.

"Hey, gang," Tarrant said, "I'm glad you were here and I want you to drive home safely. There are deer out there. If you see a deer run across the street in front of you, slow down, because a second or third deer may be right on his heels. Drive slowly until you get on the main roads. Remember there are also state troopers out there, so drive carefully." Everyone thanked Consuela and Tarrant for the wonderful evening. Nick saw his guests off and then accompanied Victoria out to Slocum's truck. Nick gave her a kiss on the cheek and a hug, helping her up and into the back seat of the truck. He then helped Karin into the front passenger seat. He and Slocum gave each other a bear hug.

"You were on your best behavior tonight," Slocum said. "You didn't argue with anyone. You may be losing your touch!"

Nick was back up near his front door when Slocum's truck pulled down the long, winding driveway behind the cars of the other guests. The departing vehicles looked like a convoy moving out. The electric gate whirred open and then closed after the guests drove to get onto the main road. Nick waited until he no longer heard Slocum's big truck engine fading in the distance.

It was completely quiet at Fort Apache.

Back in the house, Consuela was in the great room picking up the cups and glasses. She already had the dining room cleaned up. Nick walked in blowing into his cold hands and offered to help.

Consuela dismissed him with a wave. "I've got it all under control, Señor Nick. You relax and I'll see you in the morning."

She finished up and excused herself, saying she was going off to bed.

Nick told her she had done a super job.

# CHAPTER TWELVE

**N**ick was sitting in one of the easy chairs paging through a magazine when, at 11:30 p.m., his cell phone rang. He immediately thought it was one of his guests calling to say they had an unexpected run-in with Bambi or another member of the deer family. Nick did not recognize the incoming number.

"Hello?"

"Nick, this is a call from a member of the old gray-beard network. It's Rusty Dillon. I apologize for calling this late but we urgently need to talk. Urgently…like soonest… like tonight! I know your guests are all now gone so I'll be at your gate in ten minutes. Let me in and we'll pow-wow!"

The call cut off.

Nick had not heard from Rusty Dillon for nearly four years. They were friends and Agency professionals, former members of the CIA's Special Activities Division. Dillon did not waste his time, and if he wanted to talk at this time of night without any earlier notification or preamble, it had to be something extremely important.

Nick went into his downstairs study and checked his security cameras.

Ten minutes later a motorcycle pulled up to the front gate. The biker lifted his helmet visor and leaned over to speak into the box as he pushed the button on the gate's side console.

"You know who, Nick. I'm here to talk."

Nick remotely opened the gate and the motorcycle came down the winding driveway. Nick went out into the hallway and opened the front door. Rusty Dillon was already off his bike and taking off his helmet, which he hung on the handlebars. He ran both hands through his long hair and came up the front steps to the open front door where Nick stood waiting. Only minutes earlier Nick had advised Consuela on the intercom that he had an old friend coming in for a late visit but that this friend was just stopping by while in the neighborhood and they would not need anything.

Rusty and Nick shook hands and bear hugged at the front door. Rusty came and unzipped his leather Harley jacket, shrugged it off, and laid it down on the floor near the door.

"I can hang that up," said Nick.

"No, it's all good and I'll be able to find it if we have too much to drink and I'm crawling out."

Rusty was a highly respected and experienced special-operations officer who had started his career as a Green Beret in Vietnam before joining the Agency in the late '60s. He was a natural leader who quickly earned the respect of his people. He was an unflappable operations officer who handled issues with a cool demeanor and serious business manner. His fingerprints were all over any major clandestine special-operation run by the Agency in the last several decades. In one word, Dillon was a pro, and you wanted him next to you if you were going into harm's way. He was loyal, determined, and highly skilled. Dillon did not play games when running operations and he, like a number of others in the Special Activities Division, suffered no fools. One had to earn Dillon's respect, but once you did, he had your back and would defend you for making a last-minute decision to change an operational plan. In brainstorming meetings, Dillon was always a gentleman who listened well and used a great deal of common sense in putting together a special-operational plan. His was the key vote on the final decision to go or not to go ahead with the operation. Rusty Dillon was anything but a "cowboy" even though he rode motorcycles, jumped out of airplanes, practiced martial arts, and ran in Iron Man hundred-mile races. People paid close attention to what he had to say.

Nick had not seen Rusty since he had retired from the Agency. Mutual friends in the "gray-beard brotherhood" would pass along any scuttlebutt about where people were living, what they were doing, who they were dating or divorcing, and what they were bagging when out hunting or fishing. Nick had heard Rusty first went out to the Southwest but later heard he was somewhere down in the Florida Keys. There was also some buzz that Rusty was out in the Middle East on a security contract. Whatever he was doing, he was doing it very quietly and off the screens of anyone in the Washington circles who thrived on taking notes and gossiping.

"Hey, buddy, great seeing you!" said Nick. "When did'ja buy your Harley Lowboy? We've got a lot to catch up on. Come in and get warm. What would you like to drink? Why don't you spend the night? I've got plenty of room."

"No, Nick, I can't, but let's start with a drink. What're you offering?"

Nick went over to the small bar just off the great room. "Let's start with some Irish whiskey on ice. Grab one of those big chairs and relax. When did'ja get up in the area and how long you staying? You look well."

Rusty grinned. "They warn people working in hospitals never to tell someone they look well because you never know what's really going on with them or what medical problems they're facing. So let's just say I'm hanging in there."

Rusty still looked fit and trim. His hair was long but he really had not changed. There were additional crow's feet around his eyes and the scar on the bridge of his nose was still noticeable. He was tan and his eyes were clear.

Rusty sat down and spread out his legs in front of him. "Just passing through and won't be here long." Rusty was in jeans, riding boots, and a black sweatshirt with the word *Honor* emblazoned on the left front side of it.

Nick brought over the glasses and handed one to Rusty before sitting down in the other large easy chair. He raised his glass. "To good-looking women everywhere!" They raised their glasses and took a drink.

"You just missed Slocum by an hour," Nick said. "He would've loved to see you."

Rusty nodded. "I know. We saw him leave with your other guests."

"We?" Nick echoed. "What's going on? Why were you watching the house? And why didn't you just stop by to see me when Slocum was here?"

"I'm going to get to all that after you put on some background music to keep our conversation a bit more private." He was alluding to sound masking, Lesson 101 in the trade craft bible.

Nick went over to the stereo and put on steel-drum calypso music. He came back and sat down. "Now you have my full attention. What's up?"

Rusty lifted his glass. "Here's to the good guys, and to put it politely, piss on the bad guys!"

They both took a drink before Rusty lowered his glass. "Nick, tonight's conversation never took place. Everything you hear tonight you did not hear from me. What I'm going to tell you tonight will make some things a lot clearer for you and maybe help you connect the proverbial dots in some of the things you have recently been interested in. We're aware you've been asking questions while trying to help an FBI friend with some issues he's wrestling with and trying to resolve."

Rusty waited a moment and then smiled. "How many times in the intel community world have we heard someone say that we need to connect the dots?"

Rusty stretched his legs and held the boots up and off the rug for about thirty seconds without saying another word. Nick just watched his face and said nothing.

Rusty brought both boots down on the floor. "Nick, let me repeat my opener that we've never talked tonight. After I leave tonight, you may never see me again. That's if I don't want to see you. It will be impossible to find me if I don't want you to. I might be in South America, Mexico, the Florida Keys, or Texas. I might be under an alias, false ID, driver's license, passport, and anything else I need to stay off the radar screen. I'll leave no tracks and will have enough trip wires set up out there that I'll know if someone is looking for me. And who knows? Maybe with a bit of time I might even succumb in my cage-match battle with an Agent Orange issue from my days in Vietnam. If so, I'll have had my ticket punched already and moved to the other side." He laughed. "And try to find me there!"

Rusty had not changed his tone and continued with a matter-of-factly calm voice. He looked directly at Nick. "The bottom line is that you'll never find me if I don't want you to, so don't even waste your time. Full copy?"

Nick nodded. "Full copy, but what the hell is going on?"

"You've been asking a lot of mutual contacts in the old crowd at the Agency and Pentagon if anyone had any insights on playing cards left at two crime scenes here in the Washington area."

Nick's eyes widened. "I've been asking about playing cards but haven't talked about any crime scenes. You obviously know something about what's going on, so I hope you're here to talk to me about the two recent murders the FBI is now investigating. What do you know about the murder of Ed Pierce and the guy from NSA? Are you involved?"

Rusty lifted his empty glass. "How about a refill?"

He handed his glass to Nick, who walked over to the bar and put more ice in the glass before bringing it back along with the bottle of Irish whiskey. Nick sat down and poured both of them refills, setting the bottle on the nearby table.

Nick's mind was racing. Rusty never pulled punches and he clearly had something important to say.

"Don't tell me you're involved in these murders or that any of the old gang might be involved. What do you know about the murders?"

Rusty took a long drink. "I'm not here to talk to you about murders, and I'm certainly not here to tell you I've been involved in murdering anyone. I'm here to talk to you about a special operation, a covert action, a psy-op. This is about winning the hearts and minds of American citizens; it's not about murders.

"You've been out checking the rat lines on anyone having any information about the Pierce and Pagelli deaths. We'll get to those issues in a few minutes. Let me start with a journalist you might know or have heard of. Mr. Stephen Craig of the *Washington Gazette Bugle* has, on any number of occasions, written stories from anonymous government sources who have leaked classified information about special operations. He's a poster boy for the freedom of the press and free speech defenders. He stands on his public soap box and claims he will go to jail before revealing his source of classified information. He appoints himself the judge and jury about releasing secrets and weakening national security, going about his newspaper business as if he carries no responsibility for leaking these secrets. He considers himself above the pain and agony, suffering, sacrifice, and loss of risk takers in the operational world. There're no secrets in Craig's world, just the breaking news in his stories with his byline and growing fame of being a Washington insider."

Nick was now leaning forward in his chair listening to every word. His eyes were wide open and looking directly at Rusty. "I just saw a brief article on a back page of the *Gazette Bugle* stating that Craig was recovering from a stroke in the Washington Rehab Center."

Rusty took a drink and set down his glass. "I saw the same article. Craig is a punk-ass hack who has come close to committing treason with a number of his articles based on leaks of classified information. He is ego driven and overly ambitious. He thinks nothing of divulging operational secrets and seems to have no qualms when challenged. He quickly defends his actions by saying that the American public has a right to know what's going on. Craig feels that everything's on the table when discussing international and world affairs. He takes no sides, especially not the US side, and works every day to find out more government secrets. Folks in the black-ops and special-operations world bust their asses and put their lives at risk to carry out these operational missions, only to have Mr. Asshole lay out operational details in one of his gotcha articles in his newspaper. Then he takes the high road up bullshit mountain when someone challenges him on his source of the classified information. He gets up on the soapbox and says he can never reveal the identity of his source. His last front-page exposé to advance his career was about a US-Saudi black op in Yemen. He and his anonymous source laid out the details of a targeting op to take out several terrorist leaders who were planning operations to kill Americans in the US embassy. His story revealed classified information that these targets, who were Shia leaders in Yemen with close affiliation with Iran, were being targeted. The targets were all trained in Iran and supplied with Iranian weapons."

Rusty looked angry. He locked his jaw and looked down at his boots. He took a big swig of his drink and looked at Nick. "Craig's spin was that this action to take them out would embroil the United States further in the regional conflict between Iran and Saudi Arabia and put us on the side of the Sunni in the religious war against the Shia. What the asshole didn't know, or it didn't matter even if he knew, was that we lost two special operators getting these targets into our sights. The op was given a stand-down order when the article came out on the front page of the *Gazette Bugle*. The terrorist targets immediately went to ground and we had to start all over again to track them. The good guys were all set to rid the world of these scumbags only to be told to go back to the drawing board and start over."

Rusty poured himself a third glass of Irish whiskey and took another swig. "Given what we already paid in dues with the two dead special operators, some of the guys were understandably pissed. So they, and let's use that pronoun instead of 'we,' arranged a private chin-wag with Mr. Craig. They persuaded him to give them the name of his source of classified information, promising him they'd just have a quiet discussion with the source about his wrongdoing. Craig sensed it was better to give them the name of his source rather than piss them off. That source was Ed Pierce."

Nick felt he had been kicked in the stomach and hit in the head with a bat. He had known Pierce for years and would never have thought he would have been so cavalier about releasing classified information to the press.

Flabbergasted, Nick asked, "So what did they do with Ed's name?"

"So they go to see our old buddy Ed for a 'counseling session,' to warn him to knock off playing any other games. Ed gets huffy and tells them he is going to report them for making the outrageous charge that he'd leaked classified information. They don't tell Ed they've already talked to Mr. Asshole, who gave them his name, so they just let Ed blather on. Ed starts to overplay his hand, however, when he threatens to contact the FBI and report them. They tried in vain to convince him that he might find himself in trouble with the FBI for leaking classified information to the press, but he tells them to get screwed and repeats his threat to go to the authorities."

Rusty paused and took a long pull on his drink. "Things went downhill real fast when one of the visitors asked Pierce if he had received any money for the leaked information. Ed went, as they say, bat shit, so they ended the conversation once and for all. They plugged the leak and left a warning note with the body. Ed Pierce never admitted he had provided information to Craig but the visitors were convinced they had to do something or Pierce would report them to the authorities."

Nick still could not believe what he was hearing. To think Ed Pierce would leak classified information was unbelievable. But Rusty Dillion was a truth teller who told it like it was with no spin or nuance.

"And the ten of spades?" asked Nick.

"You know why special operators leave a card on a target," said Rusty.

"Did these folks go back to Craig after they dealt with Pierce?"

"They did, but only to let Craig know they had tried to talk sense into Pierce and in the end had no other alternative but to deal with him. They also informed Craig that his days of leaking classified information were over, and if he stepped across the line they would visit his family and then him. Craig was now a true believer and knew he was toast if he ever published classified information."

"Did that pressure lead to his stroke?"

Rusty showed no remorse. "Maybe yes, maybe no, but they didn't do anything else to cause the stroke. It may be that Craig's climb up the ladder to fame is over, however. He's in a wheelchair and unable to communicate. His younger and very pretty wife is already running around after only a couple of weeks with a real estate broker from the tennis club in Potomac. The Craigs have two kids. The son has an opioid drug problem and the younger daughter is driving around much too fast in her father's new BMW. She is a menace to herself and others. There are a lot of loose ends in the Craig tribe, and another chapter in living the American dream."

"What can you tell me about the jack of spades left with the warning on the Pagelli body?"

"Well, that's a different situation. In that case, someone else inside the government, not one of our guys, got word that Mr. Pagelli was leaking. He had served with NSA on TDYs in both Iraq and Afghanistan. The guy who blew the whistle on him worked closely with NSA and began to get suspicious after seeing stories in the press about US policy against the Taliban in Afghanistan. These were all front-page stories in the *Washington Gazette Bugle*, all written by the same female journalist. Pagelli was put under a micro-scope and those suspecting him began to monitor carefully his mind-set and activity.

"In many ways he was a bit of a strange duck. His claim to fame outside the office was that he was an amateur chef. At first, those suspecting him worried that Pagelli was work-ing for a foreign government. A couple of them knew him from his overseas assignments. Then it all apparently came together when they read one of the *Gazette Bugle* stories on

Taliban cross-border operations from an anonymous source who was not officially authorized to discuss the material in the article. The *Gazette* journalist was Janet Kellog, a leftist journalist who is a strong believer in globalism. She is also a strong advocate for sanctuary cities and protection of illegal immigrants. The article that raised the antenna was one by Kellog dealing with plans to target Taliban leadership near the Afghan border with Pakistan. They started to watch Kellog and her movements, thinking she might be in contact with a foreign intel service. She then wrote another article about secretive black-ops spending programs in Afghanistan and they figured they needed to step up and do something. They established that Kellog and Pagelli were in social contact, even lived on the same street. Some of the guys thought he might be banging her, but the more they looked into it they found that the connection, at least on the surface, was about friendship, private dinners, and cooking. They then thought it was more than coincidental that Kellog wrote several lead stories about FISA coverage and the unmasking of American government officials. The more they put the two of them under the microscope, the more they became convinced Pagelli was her anonymous source on black-operations and FISA leaks. Within a short time frame of watching them closely and even putting a bug in Kellog's house, they confirmed that Pagelli was providing her with classified information for her front-page *Gazette Bugle* stories."

Rusty picked up his glass, looked into it, then set it back down. "Kellog was a favorite of Pagelli's and was flattered by her attention. He would talk freely with her about any question she asked about what was going on in Iraq and Afghanistan. They often met alone at her house, and over time she even got him talking about FISA operations."

Rusty picked up his glass and swirled the whiskey around before taking a drink. He set the glass back down and waved off Nick, who had picked up the bottle and was going to pour him another drink.

"No thanks, I'm good." He paused a moment and then went on. "So 'they' made a morning visit to Pagelli, who was getting ready to leave for work. One of the guys he knew and had worked with in Iraq knocked on his door and Pagelli let him and another guy in. They confronted him and accused him of providing classified information to Janet Kellog. They wanted to know why he was doing this and asked if he didn't think what he was doing was damaging national security.

"Pagelli took his two visitors on the bullshit magic carpet ride just like Pierce about who today keeps secrets, everyone leaks, leaking is as old as baseball, what damage is really done, American citizens have the right to know, yadda, yadda. His trite explanation that this is the way things are done today in Washington started to grate on the two visitors. Pagelli said if leaking was really a crime and taken seriously in Washington, why wouldn't the FBI and Justice Department be finding out and prosecuting leakers. No names of leakers ever surfaced and no follow-up was ever made. He said the leaked information in today's newspaper is long forgotten by the end of the week when another story probably based on more or new classified information is leaked by yet another anonymous source who's not authorized to discuss information about government plans or ongoing operations. Pagelli asked what was wrong with it since the government itself leaks information all the time, and the same's true in Congress, where politicians go after political foes by leaking damaging information on them. With few exceptions, no one's ever caught being the source for leaking information."

Visibly angry, Rusty folded his hands together. "It was when Pagelli started to tell them he was going to call Janet Kellog and advise her to go to the authorities that his visitors decided to tie up this loose end before he could do any more damage. One of the guys said Pagelli was doing all this damage with his eyes wide open, so the visitors just closed them for him."

Rusty locked his jaws and grimaced. "There was also talk about a visit to Kellog. They've been thinking she clearly was manipulating a lonesome Pagelli and using him to get classified information. This would not have been difficult given Pagelli's views about leaking. They decided to hold off because two homicides on the same street in a quiet neighborhood would cause too much of a stir. So the journalist has a pass, at least for the time being."

Nick looked hard at his old friend. "Tell me, Rusty, were you at the houses when these guys were murdered? Did you participate in the decision to kill them?"

"There you go again, Nick, talking about murders when I'm talking about a psy-op and covert action to change people's way of thinking about the risk of committing treason. This was about wanting to win the hearts and minds of people and make them understand that leaking classified information undermines national security. It is not a game and you know that. The visitors wanted to put down a marker that someone leaking information would be doing so now at their own risk. They hoped that other people playing games would think twice before stepping across the line and breaking the law. They also wanted to send an important message to the newspapers, to the government, and to Congress, that leaking information can be risky, and those leaking information might be held accountable. Do you think classified information is leaked in Moscow, Beijing, Teheran, or Damascus? How about leaks in Caracas or Havana? The answer is obviously no, and both Pierce and Pagelli would be alive today if they had only listened."

Rusty began rubbing his right knee before stretching it out and moving it back and forth. "This getting old bullshit is a real pain in the ass...as well as the knees." He stopped talking while he worked out the stiffness in his leg.

Tarrant waited while mulling everything over in his head. Who were the actual killers? Were they from one group of special operators or a mixture of special-operator friends? Were they still in government service or now off the reservation and acting as self-appointed vigilantes and enforcers? Did the group have a name? Was it a club of rogue warriors? Who called the shots and selected targets? And when might they make their next visit to a leaker? Tarrant remained silent.

"So these fellows took action," Rusty said, "but soon realized that they were facing a conundrum...and you and I remember in the old days how much we hated that word. They weren't getting their cease-and-desist message out to those who needed to hear it. Certainly no one at the *Gazette Bugle* was getting it. The written messages and targeting cards were all in the investigators' chain of evidence from the crime scenes and not widely publicized. Their warning to others not to leak classified information was not getting out so they started to think about what to do next. How do they win the hearts and minds of those handling classified information without bringing the FBI down on them? To lay back, wait, and do nothing would risk more secrets being leaked on the front pages of a Washington, New York, or Los Angeles newspaper, and that would risk inflicting more damage to national security."

Rusty picked up the bottle but then thought better about pouring himself another drink. He gestured to Tarrant whether to pour him a refill but Tarrant shook his head.

Rusty put his glass down and sat back. "They felt no joy in taking action against those who leaked the information. They're not about killing American citizens, but they're all about defending our national security. They figured they didn't have the time to figure out in each case what the specific motive was of the person leaking the secrets. It could be money, revenge, moral outrage, career advancement, ego, whatever. It also could be because the person leaking the secrets is a tool of a foreign government trying to drive a stake into our national security.

"American citizens today have no idea of the danger from foreign intelligence services using leaked information to gain advantage over our country. The powers that be don't even consider that a journalist knowingly or unknowingly might be used as a covert-action agent for a foreign service. This would be unthinkable because in the Washington mind-set journalists can't be spies or agents of influence. Journalists wrap themselves in the cloak of American liberties and freedoms. They are above the fray and interested only in their claim to be seeking the truth. Independent journalism and truth." Rusty snorted in derision. He lifted his palm upward in a dismissive gesture and then lowered it. "But we know for a fact that our enemies all the time are in the recruitment business and looking for assets to carry out their bidding. The person or persons carrying out their objectives may never even know they are being used as pawns by foreign enemies. Couldn't happen here in America, but it could happen to a journalist anywhere else in the world? Yeah, right!"

Nick just sat there listening to every word Rusty was saying. He was dumbfounded. He thought he probably personally knew, if not knew of, some of the "action team" members involved in the murders, but he knew them only to be patriots who had made great sacrifices in the past to defend America. He also understood there were times in special operations when you did what you had to do. What he was now hearing felt like a ticking time bomb put in his lap.

"Soon after you started to run the rat lines with questions about the use of targeting cards, these operators figured you were somewhat aware of what happened to Pierce, and maybe even Pagelli," Rusty said. "They brainstormed to make a decision about what they should do next. As I already mentioned, they don't get off on killing American citizens, so they decided to have me come by and chat with you entirely off the record. That's why I'm here tonight."

"What do you want me to do?" asked Nick.

"Well, since we never had this conversation, I would suggest that anything you say as you move forward needs to be based only on your speculation and conjecture. You'll be guessing and theorizing and your suggestions will all be based only on your 'thinking out of the box.' For your own piece of mind, let me say that I was not involved directly with the decision to deal with Pierce or Pagelli. I don't bullshit, as you know. I'm simply the mouthpiece selected to come and talk with you. While I didn't make the decisions to plug the leaks, I understand why they did. They want to get the word out that you can be held accountable for leaking classified information, and you do so at your own risk."

Tarrant nodded. "I hear you loud and clear, but in my mind I'm already thinking about how to convince Doc Holliday and the FBI that I'm only conjecturing."

"Nick, you're too smart an operator not to figure out how you lead the horse to water and get Holliday to at least begin to look at how the two scenarios are connected," said Dillon. "Maybe he pulls Janet Kellog aside and puts her under oath before asking if Pagelli was her last anonymous source for the article about Afghanistan or the FISA disclosures. Holliday can insinuate that he found something at Pagelli's home to base his question on. Even if she is with a lawyer from the *Gazette Bugle,* she and her lawyer will realize that at this time she has little to gain withholding information that might be in some way connected to the killing. She cannot play her freedom of the press card in a homicide investigation for fear she might be implicated in Pagelli's demise. I'm not a lawyer but I would think the targeting card left at the scene would convince her that she should play ball and maybe even get protection."

Rusty took a deep breath. "Even if at first she doesn't believe she could have a problem, she may have a second thought because of Pagelli's brutal death, and this may at least have her think twice before publishing her next story based on classified information. But maybe not. Maybe she's another person who thinks there are no secrets worth keeping and everyone plays the leak game. If so, she would be wise to know that her side door needs a dead bolt installed, and that she should not walk her pet poodle, Milo, down by the brook in the early evening. And maybe she better start checking under her Toyota Avalon before starting it."

Tarrant shook his head. "Don't do anything to her until I get a chance to think about how I'll handle this. We don't need another body with another playing card and warning message." He rubbed his temples. "I've got to figure out how my conjecture to the FBI about connecting the dots and showing both men were guilty of leaking classified information doesn't bring them right to my doorstep and make them think I'm somehow involved."

"First, both of the victims were breaking secrecy laws," Rusty pointed out. "Second, if you were involved with either case, why would you conjecture about a motive that then would immediately bring suspicion on you? Third, how did you even know some of the crime scene details? Fourth, what proof do they have against you? You knew Pierce but had not seen him for years. You never met Pagelli, and you've had nothing to do with the screaming leftist agenda journalists from the *Gazette Bugle*.

"And we've never had this conversation because I've got an airtight alibi that I'm on a fishing boat right now off the coast of Louisiana."

Both men sat there looking at each other. Tarrant was trying to digest all that he had just heard and trying to get his mind around what he had to do next.

"Just FYI," Rusty spoke up, "this is all strictly compartmented in the black-ops world and the names of the guys playing off the reservation will never be known. If they have to take another action, they will, but this time to make their point, they'll probably visit both the source of the leaks and the journalist. The crime scenes will be left spotless but their next message may have to be more pointed about what's troubling them. Everyone hopes this will not be necessary. So you see, they're trying to save another life by asking me to come by and talk with you tonight."

Rusty stood up and stretched. "Any questions, Nick? I've got to hit the road. It was great seeing ya, and I do apologize for leaving all this at your doorstep. Don't even try to find me, and remember, I'll know if you do. This is about protecting our country and attaching accountability to those playing games and endangering the security of our nation. The lightweights in the Justice Department have piss-poor batting averages in ever finding people who leak information. They simply drive their feeble efforts out into the dense political fog of Washington politics and never get to the bottom of anything."

Rusty got up and headed toward the front door where he picked up his leather motorcycle jacket off the floor.

"Rusty, how do I contact you?" Nick asked.

"You don't, Nick. Unless there's something new and troublesome, I won't be back on your screen. Do us all a favor and get this message out. There are secrets that need to be protected. Leaking classified information is not a game to be played when national security is at risk. People in both government and journalism need to be held accountable, because some of these leaks border on treason. It's not a political game to be played by amateurs."

Rusty zipped his jacket and opened the front door. He and Nick hugged each other on the front porch.

"Stay well, brother, and ride safe," said Nick, who hoped this was not the last time he saw Rusty Dillon.

"Great seeing you, Nick. Take care." Rusty put on his helmet and leather gloves, got on the Harley, and turned on the engine that growled its loud roar.

Rusty waved before pulling down his visor and putting the bike in first gear. Nick smiled when he noticed there was no license plate on the back of the bike.

He opened the gate automatically from inside the front door and stayed on the porch as Dillon ran through the gears. The gate was now closed and the Harley engine noise had faded away. It was completely quiet.

# CHAPTER THIRTEEN

**N**ick did not sleep well. He kept running over in his mind all that Dillon had told him. He couldn't get over the shock that Ed Pierce had leaked classified information to Craig at the *Gazette Bugle*. He'd nod off only to be awake in twenty minutes. At about 5:00 a.m., he got up and went into the study. He had to think.

At 8:00 a.m. he called Slocum and said he was coming into town later that morning and they needed to have a private discussion. When Slocum asked what it was about, Nick simply told him it was urgent. Slocum didn't ask any more questions.

"I'll be in the man cave with coffee ready," he said simply.

In spite of all the stress he was under, Nick called Victoria on the ride into town. "I hope I'm not waking you."

She laughed. "I was already out walking my dog and now I'm unpacking a few final things from my move. Thank you for the spectacular dinner last night. I am most impressed with Consuela. She is such a wonderful person and a great cook."

Nick told her he was already on the road and she sounded pleased that he was coming into town.

"Is everything all right?" she asked.

It might have been his voice that sounded troubled but he brushed her question aside, telling her all was good.

"Can I take you to lunch after my meeting with Slocum?"

"I have an even better idea. Why don't you and Slocum come by my place for lunch?"

"Sounds good. We will be over by early afternoon."

Nick got to Slocum's house a little before 10:00 a.m. and went directly to the man cave.

Slocum opened the door and play-grumbled about being pulled out of bed so early to answer Nick's call. He handed Nick a cup of coffee. "This call to battle stations better be good."

Nick sat down across from Slocum and took a drink of the bitter brew. "That will all depend on your definition of good. Turn on some music."

Nick got right to the point. "The conversation I'm now going to have with you is between us only. You have protected my butt any number of times over a full career, and I'm now going to pay you back and protect you." He took a deep breath. "Last night shortly after everyone left the party I got a late-night visit at the house from someone you and I both know. I won't tell you the name of the visitor to protect you. If we ever are standing before a judge and jury defending ourselves against charges of being accessories to murder, you can honestly say you didn't and still don't know who the visitor was. You may one day thank me for keeping you in the dark."

Slocum simply nodded, indicating he understood.

"My late-night visitor let me know he was aware that I've been out checking rat lines and asking questions about execution-style killings involving a .22 caliber weapon, as well as playing cards. He said he knew I was also fishing for the motive behind the killings. He then said he was visiting to give me answers to my questions. According to him, both Pierce and Pagelli were guilty of leaking classified information to the *Washington Gazette Bugle*.

"He claimed both men were killed only after ignoring warnings to stop their reckless actions. Some of the things they said pissed off the people who had paid them a visit with the express purpose to warn them to cease and desist.

Neither Pierce nor Pagelli apparently showed any remorse for their actions and gave the visitors the impression that they were prepared to report the visitors to federal authorities. Whatever was said, and maybe it was this last piece about threatening to report them, something tipped the scales, and the decision was made to take the leakers out."

Rapt, Slocum listened carefully to every word.

"The message last night from this guy to me, and now from me to you, is that we need to get the word out that leaking classified information to the press can be, shall we say, dangerous to your health. To quote him, he said leaking is not a game and secrets need to be protected. He also said it's not dependent on your mood swing that day, or your views about political decisions being made or not made, or your friendship with a journalist, or a journalist's career advancement. It's about risking our national security.

"There was more. To quote my visitor, he said that the people who think leaking is the new norm, and the way things are done today in Washington, is bullshit. He claimed these leaks are coming from rookies and amateurs who have little experience in security matters. Professionals in the intelligence community and the special-operations world are unable to explain how this practice of leaking goes on. These professionals become even more skeptical when no one is ever found to be responsible for leaking the secret information. The game goes on unchecked and journalism gets away with all it can to sell newspapers without doing a counterintelligence scrub and asking questions about protecting national security. He said this is naïve. The newspaper editors, journalists, and leakers don't even think it's possible that a foreign intelligence service could be somehow connected behind the scenes to the leaks of classified information. These same naïve people apparently underestimate that these foreign intelligence services are always out there looking to recruit new sources and influence US government matters."

Nick stopped talking and took a minute to recall what else he wanted to tell Slocum about the late-night visitor.

"My visitor told me in strong terms what we already know: that the people involved in leaking classified information are breaking the law and endangering national security. He suggested that if the government cannot find out who is involved in the leaks, maybe someone else can find out and do something about it. He said those involved in taking action against the two leakers don't get off by killing US citizens. As proof, he said that's why they left the warnings to cease and desist."

The phone rang and Slocum answered with a grunt. He handed the phone to Nick. "It's Victoria." Slocum got up to get more coffee.

"I saw your car outside and just wanted to know what time to have lunch ready," Victoria said.

"Bill and I will be over right at one p.m."

"Great, I'll see you then."

Nick ended the call. "We're invited to Victoria's for lunch at thirteen hundred hours. I've been up most of the night thinking about what we do next. We have raised our hands and pledged to defend our country and constitution. It's about honor, integrity, and core values. We pledged to uphold the law and can't just sit on the sidelines and watch these vigilantes take their own action to stop the leaking of classified information. You don't *break* the law to *defend* the law. These people think they're on the side of justice and the two targets down are simply collateral damage. They think they're taking direct action to plug leaks and protect national security while sending out a message that anyone who leaks information does so at their own risk. These people are pros and wrapped in the American flag and patriotism. They love America.

"We need to do all we can to avoid a third victim. I'm going to lay out to Doc Holliday what the two killings are all about and let the FBI figure out how they can get a warning out to government employees that leaking classified information in the future can get you killed. The new word in the equation is *risk*!"

Slocum nodded in agreement. "How you gonna do that without telling Doc who your late-night visitor was?"

"Yeah, that's going to be the tricky part. I've given it a lot of thought. Here's what I think has to be done..."

Nick turned up the background music on the radio, then walked back over and sat down. He leaned in close to Slocum and, in a low, soft voice, laid out the plan.

At 12:50 p.m. Nick told Slocum to go across to Victoria's while he made a phone call to confirm a dinner invitation he made for that same night at a neighbor's house near Fort Apache. He said he would be over soon.

Slocum put on his jacket. "I'll see you over there."

Twenty minutes later, Nick was at Victoria's front door. She opened it with a great smile on her face. She looked stunning in jeans and a cotton shirt.

"You clearly are looking too healthy after last night's dinner and drinks," he remarked.

She grinned. "A compliment like that will get you a free lunch, Tarrant. Thanks again for last night's wonderful dinner. I had great fun and your house is awesome. It's right out of *House Beautiful*."

She motioned him to follow her into the house. "I'm serving lunch in the glass-enclosed sunroom in the back of the house just off the kitchen."

Slocum was already seated and picked up on Nick's quick nod that the plan was a go. Afterward, a meeting with Holliday would be arranged.

Lunch was good. Victoria served them homemade onion soup and grilled ham-and-cheese sandwiches, followed by slices of delicious pound cake.

At the first opportunity, Nick asked if Victoria would be interested in coming out the following weekend and staying at his house. He'd also be inviting Slocum and Karin.

"I could teach you how to shoot a bow and arrow, or we could go hiking or biking." He quickly added he would be just as happy if she only wanted to spend the time talking and relaxing in the heated pool and Jacuzzi. "If you wanted, we also could visit one or two of the local restaurants near the house. Both places are known for providing good dinners and friendly atmospheres."

"It sounds great," Victoria said, "but I have to take care of my dog."

"Bring the dog out with you. There are good trails on my property and in the nearby state park, and the dog could get plenty of exercise."

She flashed that great smile. "Then I would be delighted to come."

"Karin and I will also definitely be there," Slocum said. He looked at his watch. "It's three o'clock. I have to get going."

"Why the rush?" Nick asked.

"I made a commitment to a friend to help him move some things into storage."

On Slocum's way out, Nick said, "I'll see you during the week when Doc Holliday can get away for a meeting."

Slocum thanked Victoria. "Karin and I are looking forward to the upcoming weekend at Fort Apache."

Nick helped Victoria clean up the dishes from lunch. Over coffee in the living room, they talked about her classes, the difficulties in a move to a new house and starting a new job, and how the dog was slowly adjusting to the new environs.

"May I ask you a question?" Victoria said and Nick nodded. "When you didn't come in with Bill, I asked him where you were? He said you were making a call about some wetwork repair that needed to be done. What was he talking about?"

Nick smiled. "'Wetwork' is a Russian euphemism used for spilling of blood, murder, or the assassination of enemies. At one time, the KGB had a Department 13, which was known as the Department of Wet Works.

"You told me that you like to watch old movies. If you go back to *The Eiger Sanction*, with a young Clint Eastwood, you'll see them talking about assassination, murder, or 'wetwork' being planned by some bad guys. Wetwork is a euphemism in Russian that is well understood. It is also a well-known term in the big eastern American cities as a street slang term for taking somebody out, and maybe then hiding the body. Ask a guy in Brooklyn, Newark, or Philly about 'wetwork' and you'll probably hear a rendition of 'Hey, man, I don't know nothin'!'"

Victoria chuckled.

"Bill was more than likely making some theatrical reference to our efforts trying to help out our FBI friend who is investigating two recent murders. Unfortunately, there's little we can do to shed light on the killings."

Victoria sensed not to press and seemed satisfied with his answer. "I'll order up *The Eiger Sanction* on Netflix."

She then talked a bit about an issue with an obstreperous student in one of her classes who was challenging her with questions about modern science theories. She felt like he was checking out her teaching bona fides. Nick surmised it was not surprising that a student was checking her out, but probably not her credentials, however. He knew she could handle it.

A little after 5:00 p.m. Nick reluctantly told Victoria, "I have to get going because I'm attending a neighbor's birthday dinner this evening." He thanked her for lunch and said he was looking forward to seeing her on the weekend.

He kissed her only after asking her if she would mind. After all, he was reading three newspapers a day and knew all about the stories of women being preyed upon by men.

She said she appreciated his correctness, but certainly didn't mind. Nick held her closely and kissed her.

# CHAPTER FOURTEEN

A t exactly 11:00 a.m. on Monday, Tarrant knocked and was let into the man cave by Slocum. Doc Holliday was already there sitting in one of the leather chairs and drinking coffee. He had taken off both his winter coat and suit jacket and was wearing a leather shoulder holster.

Slocum handed Tarrant a cup of coffee and they both sat down.

"Okay, Mr. Clandestine Operator," Doc said, "talk to me and tell me why you pulled me over here on a workday. What'cha got?"

"Doc, I appreciate your coming over," Nick replied. "I think you'll be happy to hear what I'm going to tell you.

You know I've been out beating the bushes to come up with something about the killings. I was getting nowhere but I was out talking to a lot of folks. I asked them to put their ears to the ground and call me if they heard anything.

"For more than a week I heard nothing. Then late last night I got a call from a guy who told me he had information about the two murders. I didn't recognize the number or the voice. I tried to get his name but the guy tells me right away to keep my mouth shut and listen to what he has to say. He says he knows I've been asking around about certain police matters and that's what he wants to talk to me about. He tells me in a harsh tone that what he is going to say better be off the record. He says the deaths of Pagelli and Pierce were unfortunate but necessary since both were guilty of leaking classified information to the press. Then he said that if I didn't believe him I could ask Stephen Craig or Janet Kellog of the *Washington Gazette Bugle*, and they could tell me if his assertion was true. He said if I do talk to them at the *Bugle*, I should be sure to tell them they can thank their lucky stars they weren't targets. He and his compatriots involved in taking action are not driven by killing US citizens but are interested only in keeping secrets and protecting national security. Both Pierce and Pagelli were breaking the law and they and their newspaper editors were accessories to committing crimes. He added that it was almost a game being played out in our nation's capital. Leaked classified information is published, outrage accordingly expressed along with calls for investigations, and no one is ever found out to be the leaker. Then the cycle starts again with the next story from an anonymous source. He said they viewed this commotion and hand wringing as simply political posturing and said you can't tell us why no one seems to be able to pin the tail on the donkey and find out who is the source of the leaks.

"The guy then says he is speaking for people who now want to attach accountability to those playing this dangerous game. Leak information at your own risk. He ended by saying the feigned outrage about leaks up to now along with about five bucks can get you a Starbucks coffee. He and his colleagues are going to raise the price and change people's minds about what a leak in the future may cost the leaker."

Doc asked, "How long was the call?"

"Exactly ten minutes." Nick handed Doc a card with the incoming number written down. The number had a 301area code.

Doc glanced at the card. "Maryland. Finally, we get a break!" He got up from his chair. "I've got to get back to my office immediately but I'll contact you shortly to get a written statement."

Before Doc left the man cave, he asked Nick if he could guess who the caller was or had any idea of who might be involved.

Nick shrugged. "No, I couldn't even venture a guess."

Doc Holliday left in a rush and was already on his cell phone walking out to his car.

"Did j'a have any problems?" Nick asked Slocum.

Slocum took a drink of coffee and swallowed. "Nope. I rented a car, left all my smart phone gear behind, took a bag of change, rubber gloves, and a big hoodie, and drove over to the Eastern Shore where I found a dimly lit gas station just outside Salisbury. There was a pay phone out on one of the walls and no cameras. I made my call to you and kept the phone call going for exactly the ten minutes you told me to stay on the line. I kept rubber gloves on anytime I touched the coins and the pay phone. It was cold so I had the hoodie on and pulled over my head. No one saw me and I still had plenty of change in the bag when I finished the call. I drove back immediately after leaving the gas station. No one followed me."

"All good," said Nick. "Doc Holliday is probably confirming right now that I got a call last night that lasted for ten minutes. He'll come up empty-handed about who made the call but will know someone wanted to provide a lead to stop the killings without leaving any tracks behind.

I figure Doc'll be talking with Janet Kellog next, then the editors of the *Gazette Bugle*, who'll be speaking for Stephen Craig. I expect he'll come back to me and ask whom I've been out talking to when checking the rat lines. The fact is I've been asking questions widely across the board of special operators. Delta, Seals, Marine Raiders, Agency Special Activities, and even Secret Service, Capitol Police, and several Beltway bandit outfits. There are too many leads for him to follow and pinpoint who's pulling the trigger. Still, if he can run the lead down and charge somebody, good for him.

"So we led the horse to water and got the FBI to begin looking in the right direction about the motive for the killings. I expect they'll take measures to get the word out and warn the news folks that somebody is taking action to establish accountability for leaking classified information. I hope he leaves them with the understanding that they now leak information at their own risk."

Nick paused. "I almost think we did what the enforcers or vigilantes wanted us to do. They tried to leave warnings but the word was not getting out. They decide to hand us a ticking time bomb, knowing we would have to do something to stop a third killing. I don't know who these guys are but they're really good. Not only do they play hardball about enforcement but they screw with your mind and influence your opinion about leaking classified information. They know a lot about covert action and winning the hearts and minds of people and stopping leaks of classified information. They're letting us know that some of the leaks are close to treason, so they're changing the rules of the game. I don't know who they are but they're pulling off a hell of a covert action."

Slocum took it all in and agreed with Tarrant that these guys were really skilled in trade craft. "What more can we do?"

"We can start listening to the special-ops tom-toms about who recently lost two operatives in Yemen," Nick replied. "This may let us at least guess whom this might have royally pissed off, and that might allow us to guess who might be involved. I'm not sure we'll ever find out."

He looked at Slocum. "Bill, things have changed since we got out of the outfit. So many of our government institutions today have been politicized and are just part of the trench warfare saga between the Democrats and Republicans. There are a number of examples in the IRS, FBI, CIA, Pentagon, and the DNI, not to mention the State Department. The guys behind this covert action know that things are being done differently today, and they're not following suit. They are now taking their own action against people who are breaking the law."

Slocum nodded. "Yeah."

"I'm going home," said Nick. "Doc will be back shortly to talk to us, but what more can we really tell him?"

As he opened the door he said, "Bill, we know only too well that special operations can be complicated and at times deadly, especially when national security is involved. Some things really don't change. Maybe we just saved a life."

Nick walked to his car to start his return run to Fort Apache.

The powerful engine in the Dodge Charger was running smoothly as Nick drove west on Route 50. In his mind, he went over every word spoken in the conversation that never took place and wondered when, if ever, he would run into Rusty Dillon again.

He sure hoped Janet Kellog got the message. If not, her dog, Milo, would need to find a new home.

He smiled, knowing that Slocum would never press him to find out who his late-night visitor was. Both of them knew that at times things like this happened in special operations. Sometimes you simply don't ask questions because it's a need-to-know situation.

Nick drove about twenty minutes before starting to think about Victoria and the upcoming weekend. It might be real important to become friends with that big German shepherd.

Then he started to think again being under the man cave shower with Victoria…

Nick Tarrant was a lucky man and thought that very soon he might be even luckier.

# ABOUT THE AUTHOR

**W**illiam 'Bill' Rooney retired from the Central Intelligence Agency with more than thirty-five years of experience in the Directorate of Operations' Clandestine Service. Among other achievements in his highly successful career, he received the coveted 'Wild Bill' Donavan award and the Distinguished Career Intelligence Medal. He served a number of years overseas in foreign postings and spent a good part of his career as a senior executive in the DO. After leaving the Agency, he dedicated himself to an additional five years of working on railroad security at a time when terrorists were carrying out a series of bombing attacks against foreign rail stations and trains. Rooney wrote his first book entitled *Repeat: Whiskey Tango Foxtrot* in 2011, and currently lives with his wife in the suburbs of Washington. D.C.

# PERMUTED PRESS

needs **you** to help

# SPREAD (THE) INFECTION

## FOLLOW US!

ff | Facebook.com/PermutedPress
🐦 | Twitter.com/PermutedPress

## REVIEW US!

Wherever you buy our book, they can be reviewed! We want to know what you like!

## GET INFECTED!

Sign up for our mailing list at PermutedPress.com

**PERMUTED** PRESS

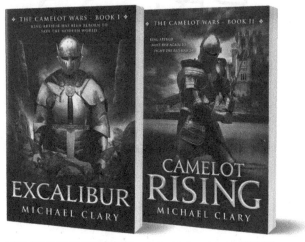

# THE ULTIMATE PREPPER'S ADVENTURE.
# THE JOURNEY BEGINS HERE!

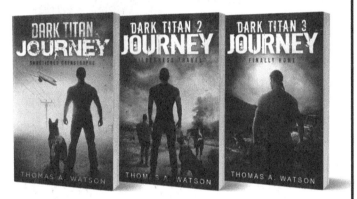

EAN 9781682611654 $9.99     EAN 9781618687371 $9.99     EAN 9781618687395 $9.99

The long-predicted Coronal Mass Ejection has finally hit the Earth, virtually destroying civilization. Nathan Owens has been prepping for a disaster like this for years, but now he's a thousand miles away from his family and his refuge. He'll have to employ all his hard-won survivalist skills to save his current community, before he begins his long journey through doomsday to get back home.

# THE MORNINGSTAR STRAIN HAS BEEN LET LOOSE—IS THERE ANY WAY TO STOP IT?

**EAN** 9781618686497  $16.00

An industrial accident unleashes some of the Morningstar Strain. The doctor who discovered the strain and her assistant will have to fight their way through Sprinters and Shamblers to save themselves, the vaccine, and the base. Then they discover that it wasn't an accident at all—somebody inside the facility did it on purpose. The war with the RSA and the infected is far from over.

This is the fourth book in Z.A. Recht's The Morningstar Strain series, written by Brad Munson.

PERMUTED
PRESS

WE CAN'T GUARANTEE THIS GUIDE WILL SAVE YOUR LIFE. BUT WE CAN GUARANTEE IT WILL KEEP YOU SMILING WHILE THE LIVING DEAD ARE CHOWING DOWN ON YOU.

**EAN** 9781618686695  $9.99

This is the only tool you need to survive the zombie apocalypse.

OK, that's not really true. But when the SHTF, you're going to want a survival guide that's not just geared toward day-to-day survival. You'll need one that addresses the essential skills for true nourishment of the human spirit. Living through the end of the world isn't worth a damn unless you can enjoy yourself in any way you want. (Except, of course, for anything having to do with abuse. We could never condone such things. At least the publisher's lawyers say we can't.)

PERMUTED
PRESS